D0294812

# About Nikki Logan

Nikki Logan lives next to a string of protected wetlands in Western Australia, with her long-suffering partner and a menagerie of furred, feathered and scaly mates. She studied film and theatre at university, and worked for years in advertising and film distribution before finally settling down in the wildlife industry. Her romance with nature goes way back, and she considers her life charmed, given she works with wildlife by day and writes fiction by night—the perfect way to combine her two loves. Nikki believes that the passion and risk of falling in love are perfectly mirrored in the danger and beauty of wild places. Every romance she writes contains an element of nature, and if readers catch a waft of rich earth or the spray of wild ocean between the pages she knows her job is done.

™

# How To Get Over Your Ex

### Nikki Logan

First published in Great Britain 2013
by Mills & Boon, an imprint of Harlequin (UK) Limited.
Harlequin (UK) Limited, Eton House, 18-24 Paradise Road,
Richmond, Surrey TW9 1SR

© Nikki Logan 2013

ISBN: 978 0 263 23423 7

Harlequin (UK) policy is to use papers that are natural, renewable and recyclable products and made from wood grown in sustainable forests. The logging and manufacturing process conform to the legal environmental regulations of the country of origin.

Printed and bound in Great Britain
by CPI Antony Rowe, Chippenham, Wiltshire

## Also by Nikki Logan

Once a Rebel…
Mr Right at the Wrong Time
Rapunzel in New York
A Kiss to Seal the Deal
Shipwrecked with Mr Wrong
Lights, Camera…Kiss the Boss!
Their Newborn Gift
Seven-Day Love Story
The Soldier's Untamed Heart
Friends to Forever

**Did you know these are also available as eBooks?**
**Visit www.millsandboon.co.uk**

*For Aaron,*
*who knows just how hard the getting over part can be.*
*Give my regards to Broadway.*

# CHAPTER ONE

*Valentine's Day 2012*

*CLOSE. Please just close.*

A dozen curious eyes followed Georgia Stone into Radio EROS' stylish elevator, craning over computer monitors or sliding on plastic floor mats back into the corridor just slightly, not even trying to disguise their curiosity. She couldn't stand staring at the back of the elevator for ever, so she turned, lifted her chin...

...and silently begged the doors to close. To put her out of her misery for just a few blessed moments.

*Do. Not. Cry.*

Not yet.

The numbness of shock was rapidly wearing off and leaving the deep, awful ache of pain behind it. With a humiliation chaser. She'd managed to thank the dumbfounded drive-time announcers—*God, she was so British*—before stumbling out of their studio, knowing that the radio station's output was broadcast in every office on every floor via a system of loudspeakers.

Hence all the badly disguised glances.

The whole place knew what had just happened to her. Because of her. That their much-lauded Leap Year Valentine's proposal had just gone spectacularly, horribly, excruciatingly, publicly wrong.

She'd asked. Daniel had declined.

As nicely as he could, under the circumstances, but his urgently whispered, "Is this a joke, George?" was still a no whichever way you looked at it and, in case she hadn't got the message, he'd spelled it out.

*We weren't heading for marriage. I thought you knew that...*

Actually no, or she wouldn't have asked.

*That's what made our thing so perfect...*

Oh. Right. *That* was what made it perfect? She'd known they were drifting in a slow, connected eddy like the leaves in Wakehurst's Black Pond but she'd thought that even drifting *eventually* got you somewhere. Obviously not.

'For God's sake, will you close?'

She wasn't usually one to talk to inanimate objects—even under her breath—but somehow, on some level, the elevator must have heard her because its shiny chrome doors started to slide together obligingly.

'Hold the lift!' a voice shouted.

She didn't move. Her stomach plunged. Just as they'd nearly closed...

A hand slid into the sliver of space between the doors and curled around one of them, arresting and then reversing its slide. They reopened, long-suffering and apologetic.

'You mustn't have heard me,' the dark-haired man said, throwing her only the briefest and tersest of glances, his lips tight. He turned, faced the front, and permitted them to close this time, giving her a fabulous view of the square cut of the back of his expensive suit.

*No,* you *mustn't have heard* me. *Making a total idiot of myself in front of all of London.* If he had, he'd have given her a much longer look. Something told her everyone would be looking at her for much longer now. Starting with all her and Daniel's workmates.

She groaned.

He looked back over his shoulder. 'Sorry?'

She forced burning eyes to his. If she blinked just once she was going to unleash the tears she could feel jockeying for expression just behind her lids. But she didn't have the heart for speech. She shook her head.

He returned his focus to the front of the elevator. She stared at the lights slowly descending toward 'G' for ground floor. Then at the one marked 'B', below that—the one he'd pressed.

'Excuse me...' She cleared her throat to reduce the tight choke. He turned again, looked down great cheekbones at her. 'Can you get to the street from B?'

He studied her. Didn't ask what she meant. 'The basement has electronic gate control.'

Her heart sank. So much for hoping to make a subtle getaway. Looked as if the universe really wanted her to pay for today's disaster.

Crowded reception it was, then.

She nodded just once. 'Thank you.'

He didn't turn back around, but his grey eyes narrowed. 'I'll be driving out through the gates. You're welcome to slip out behind me.'

*Slip* out. Was that just a figure of speech or did he know? 'Thank you. Yes, please.'

He turned back to the front, then, a heartbeat later, he turned back again. 'Step behind me.'

She dragged stinging eyes back up to him. 'What?'

'The door's going to open at Reception first. It will be full of people. I can screen you.'

Suddenly the front-line of the small army of tears waiting for a chance to get out surged forward. She fought them back furiously, totally futile.

Kindness. That was worse than blinking. And it meant that he definitely knew.

But since he was playing pretend-I-don't, she could, too. She stepped to her left just as the doors obediently opened onto the station's reception. Light and noise filled the elevator but she stood, private and protected behind the stranger, his big body as good as a locked door. She sighed. Privacy and someone to protect her—two things she'd just blown out of her life for good, she suspected.

'Mr Rush…' someone said, out in the foyer.

The big man just nodded. 'Alice. Going down?'

'No, up.'

He shrugged. 'I won't be long.'

And the doors closed, leaving just the two of them, again. Georgia sagged and swiped at the single, determined tear that had slipped down her cheek. He didn't turn back around. It took only a moment longer for the elevator to reach the basement. He walked out the moment the doors opened and reached back to hold them wide for her. The frigid outdoor air hit her instantly.

'Thank you,' she repeated and stepped out into the darkened parking floor. She'd left her coat upstairs, hanging on the back of a chair in the studio, but she would gladly freeze rather than set foot in that building ever again.

He didn't make eye contact again. Or smile. 'Wait by the gate,' he simply said and then turned to stride towards a charcoal Jaguar.

She walked a dead straight line towards the exit gate. The fastest, most direct route she could. She only reached it a moment or two before the luxury car. She stood, rubbing her prickling flesh.

He must have activated the gate from inside his vehicle, and the large, steel lattice began to rattle along rollers towards her. He nudged his car forward, lowered his window, and peered out across his empty passenger seat.

She ducked to look at him. For moments. One of them really needed to say something. Might as well be her.

'Thanks again.' *For sanctuary in the elevator. For spiriting her away, now.*

His eyes darkened and he slid designer sunglasses up onto the bridge of his nose. 'Good luck' was all he said. Then he shifted his Jag into gear and drove forward out of the still-widening gate.

She stared after him.

It seemed an odd thing to say in lieu of goodbye but maybe he knew something she didn't.

Maybe he knew how much she was going to need that luck.

*Hell.*

That was the longest elevator ride of Zander's life. Trapped in two square metres of double-thickness steel with a sobbing woman. Except she hadn't been sobbing—not outwardly—but she was hurting inwardly; pain was coming off her in waves. Totally tangible.

The waves had hit him the moment he nudged his way into her elevator, but it was too late, then, to step back and let her go down without him. Not without making her feel worse.

He knew who she was. He just hadn't known it was her standing in the elevator he ran for or he wouldn't have launched himself at the closing doors.

She must have bolted straight from the studio to the exit the moment they threw to the first track out of the Valentine's segment. Lord knew he did; he wanted to get across town to the network head offices before they screamed for him to come in.

Proactive instead of reactive. He never wanted someone higher up his food chain to call him and find him just sitting there waiting for their call. He wouldn't give them the satisfaction. Or the power.

By the time he got across London's peak-hour gridlock he'd have the right spin for the on-air balls-up. Turning a negative into a positive. Oiling the waters. The kind of problem-solving he was famous—and employed—for.

The kind of problem-solving he loathed.

He blew out a steady breath and took an orange light just as it was turning red in order to keep moving. None of them had expected the guy to say no. Who said no to a proposal, live on air? You said yes live and then you backed out of it later if it wasn't what you wanted. That was what ninety-five per cent of Londoners would do.

Apparently this guy was Mr Five Per Cent.

Then again, who asked a man to marry her live on radio if she wasn't already confident of the answer? Or maybe she thought she was? She wouldn't be the first to find out she was wrong…the hard way.

Empathy curled his fingers tight on the expensive leather of his steering wheel. Who was he to cast stones?

He'd recognised that expression immediately. The one where you'd happily agree for the elevator to plunge eight storeys rather than have to step out and face the world. At least his own humiliation had been limited to just his family and friends.

Just *two hundred* of his and Lara's nearest and dearest.

Georgia Stone's would be all over the city today and all over the world by tomorrow.

He was counting on it. Though he'd have preferred it not to be on the back of someone's pain and humiliation. He hadn't got that bad…yet.

He eased his foot onto the brake as the traffic ground to a halt around him and resisted the urge to lean on his horn.

Not that he imagined a girl like that would suffer for long. Tall and pale and pretty with that tangle of dark, short curls. She'd dressed for her proposal—that was a sweet and unexpected touch in the casual world of radio. Half his on-air staff would come to work in their pyjamas if they had the option. But Georgia Stone had worn a simple, pale pink, thin-strapped dress for the big moment—almost a wedding dress itself. If one got married on a beach in Barbados. Way too light for February so maybe public proposals weren't the only thing the pretty Miss Stone didn't think through?

Or maybe he was just looking for ways that this wasn't his fault.

He'd approved the Valentine's promotion in the first place. And the cheesy 'does your man just need a shove?' angle. But EROS' listeners were—on the whole—a fairly cheesy bunch so it had been one of their most successful promotions.

Which had made the lift ride all the more painful.

Something about her pale, wide-eyed courtesy. Even as her heart ruptured quietly in its cavity.

*Thank you.*

She'd said it four times in half the minutes. As though he were a guy just helping her out instead of the guy that put her in that position in the first place. It was his contract she'd signed. It was his station's promotion she'd put her hand up for.

Her life was now in shreds around her feet but still she thanked him.

That was one well-brought-up young woman. Youngish; he had to have at least fifteen years on her, though it was hard to know. He reached for his dash and activated the voice automation.

'Call the office,' he told his car.

It listened. 'EROS, Home of Great Music, Mr Rush's office. This is Casey, can I help you?'

Christ, he really had to have their company-wide phone greeting shortened.

'It's me,' he announced to his empty vehicle. 'I need you to pull up the contract with the Valentine's girl.'

'Just a tick,' his assistant murmured, not taking offence at his lack of acknowledgement. She knew life was too short for pleasantries. 'OK, got it. What do you need, Zander?'

'Age?'

Her silence said she was scanning the document. 'Twenty-eight.'

OK, so he had nine years on her. And her skin was amazing, then. He would have said twenty-two or -three, max. 'Duration of contract?'

Again a brief pause. 'Twelve months. To conclude with a follow-up next February fourteenth.'

Twelve months of their lives. That was supposed to include engagement party, fully paid wedding, honeymoon. All on EROS. That was the fifty-thousand-pound carrot. Why else would anyone want to make the most private, special moment of their lives so incredibly public?

The carrot was cheap in international broadcast terms, for the kind of global exposure he suspected this promo would get. Even more so now, given it had probably already gone viral. Exposure brought listeners, listeners brought advertisers, and advertisers brought revenue.

Except that follow-up twelve months from now wasn't going to make great radio. At all. His mind went straight to the weakest link.

'Casey, can you send that contract to my phone and then call Rod's assistant and let her know I'm about half an hour away?'

'Yes, sir.'

He rang off without a farewell. Life was too short for that as well.

A year was a long time to manufacture content, but if they played their cards right they could salvage something that would last longer than just the next few days. Really make that fifty thousand pounds work for them. He still expected EROS to directly benefit from the viral exposure—maybe even more now—but that contract locked them in for the next year as much as her.

A black cab cut in close to his bonnet and he gave voice to his frustration—his guilt—finally leaning on the horn the way he'd been wanting to for twenty minutes.

He spent the second half of his drive across town formulating a plan. So much so that when he walked into his network's headquarters he had it all figured out. A way forward. A way to salvage something of today's mess.

'Zander…' Rod's assistant caught his ear as he breezed past into her boss's office. He paused, turned. 'He has Nigel in there.'

Nigel Westerly. Network owner. That wasn't a good sign. 'Thanks, Claire.'

Suddenly even his salvage plan looked shaky. Nigel Westerly hadn't amassed one of the country's biggest fortunes by being easily led. He was tough. And ruthless.

Zander straightened his back.

Oh, well, if he had to be fired, he'd rather it be by one of the men he admired most in England. He certainly wasn't going to quail and wonder when the axe was going to fall. He pushed open the double doors to his director's office with flair and announced himself.

'Gentlemen…'

# CHAPTER TWO

THANK goodness for seeds. And quiet lab rooms. And high-security access passes.

Georgia's whole National Trust building was so light and bright and…optimistic. None of which she could stomach right now. Her little X-ray lab had adjustable lighting so it was dim and gloomy and could look as if she were out even when she wasn't.

Perfect.

She'd called in sick the day after Valentine's—unable to crawl out of bed was a kind of sick, right?—but she'd gone tip-toeing back to work, her Thursday and Friday an awful trial in carefully neutral smiles and colleagues avoiding eye con-tact and a very necessary and very belated inter-departmental email to Kew's carnivorous-plant department.

It was also very short.

*I'm so very sorry, Daniel. I'll miss you.*

She knew they were done. Even if Dan hadn't concurred—which he had, once he'd cooled down enough to speak to her—she couldn't spend another moment in a relationship that just drifted in small, endless circles. Not after what she'd done. Conveniently, it also meant she didn't have to explain herself, explain something she barely understood—at least not for a while. And she was nothing if not a master procrastinator. She'd see Dan eventually, apologise in person, pick up her few things from his place. But this way they were both out of their misery.

Relationship euthanasia.

You know, except for the whole intensive public interest thing...

And now it was Saturday afternoon. And work was as good a place as any to hide out from all those messages and emails from astounded friends and family. Better, probably, because there were so few staff here with her and because she worked alone in her little X-ray lab behind two levels of carded access restrictions. The world wasn't exactly interested enough in her botched proposal to have teams of paparazzi on her trail but it was certainly interested enough to still be talking about it—everywhere—a few days later. She didn't dare check her social media accounts or listen to the radio or pick up a paper in case The Valentine's Girl was still the topic de jour.

London was divided. Grand Final kind of division. Half the city had taken up arms in her defence and the other half were backing poor, beleaguered Dan. Hard to know which was worse: the flak he was copping for being the reject*or* or the abject pity she was fielding for being the reject*ee*.

*Didn't she know what a stupid thing it was to have done?* some said.

Yes, thanks. She had a pretty good idea. But it wasn't as if she just woke up one morning and wanted her face all over the papers. She'd thought he'd say yes, or she wouldn't have asked. It just turned out her inside information was about as reliable as a racing tip from some random bag lady in an alleyway.

*Why do it live on air?* her detractors cried.

Because she woke up the morning after Kelly's stunning pronouncement that her brother was ready for more and the 'Give him a Nudge' leap year promotion was all over the radio station she brushed her teeth to. And rode to work to. And did her work to. All day. The universe was practically screaming at her to throw her name into the hat.

She rubbed her throbbing temples.

*Their names.*

Dan was in it up to his neck, too, but because she wasn't about to out her best friend—for Dan's sake and for his sister's—she was still struggling with exactly what her answer would be when he eventually turned those all-seeing eyes to her and asked, *'Why, George?'*

She loaded another dish of carefully laid-out seeds into the holder and slid it into the irradiator, then secured it and moved to her computer monitor to start the X-ray. It took just moments to get a clear image. Not a bad batch; a few incompetents, like all batches, but otherwise a pretty good sample.

She typed a quick summary report of her findings, noted the low unviable percentage, and attached it to the computerised sample scan to go back to the seed checkers.

*Incompetents.* It was hard not to empathise with them, the pods that had rotten-out interiors or the husks that formed absent of the seeds they were supposed to protect. Incompetent seeds disappeared amongst the thousands of others on the plant and just never came to fruition. Their very specific genetic line simply…vanished when they failed to reproduce.

In nature, that was the end of it for them.

Incompetent seeds didn't have to justify themselves and their failure to thrive constantly to their competent mothers. Didn't have to watch their competent friends' competent families take shape and help them move out to their competent outer-city suburbs.

'Ugh…' Georgia retrieved the small sample from the irradiator, repackaged it to quarantine standards and placed it back in its storage unit. Then she reached for the next one.

Twenty-five-thousand seed species in the bank and someone had to test samples of each for viability. Lucky for the National Trust she had weeks and even months of hiding out ahead of

her. Looked as if they were going to be the immediate benefi-
ciaries of her weekends and evenings in exile.

Across the desk, her phone rang.

'Georgia Stone,' she answered, before remembering what
day it was. Why was someone calling her on a weekend?

'Ms Stone, it's Tyrone at Security. I have a visitor here for
you.'

*No. He really didn't.* 'I'm not expecting anyone. I would
have left a name.'

'That's what I told him, but he insisted.'

*Him.* Was it Daniel? Immediately, new guilt piled on top of
the old that she'd not been brave enough to face him personally yet. 'Wh...who is it?' she risked.

Pause.

'Alekzander Rush. With a *K* and a *Z*, he says.'

As if that helped her in the slightest; although some neuron
deep in her mind started firing.

'Now he says he's not a journalist.' Tyrone sounded annoyed
at being forced into the role of interpreter. His job was just to
check the ID of visitors passing through his station, not deal
with presumptuous callers.

'OK, send him through. I'll meet him in the visitor centre.
Thank you, Tyrone,' she added before he disconnected.

It took her about seven minutes to finish what she was doing,
sanitise, and work her way through three buildings to the public
visitor centre. It was teeming with weekend visitors to Wakehurst all checking out the work of her department while they
were here seeing the main house and gardens.

She glanced around and saw him. Tall, dark, and casually
but warmly dressed, with something draped over his arm. The
guy from the elevator at the radio station. Possibly the last
person in the world she expected to see. Relief that he wasn't
some crazy out to find The Valentine's Girl crashed into curiosity about why he would be here. She ignored two speculative glances sent her way by total strangers. Probably trying

to work out why she looked familiar. Hopefully, she'd be back in her office by the time the light bulb blinked on over their heads and they remembered whatever social media site they'd seen her on.

She walked up next to him as he stared into one of the public displays reading the labels and spoke quietly. 'Alekzander with a *K* and a *Z*, I assume?'

He turned. His eyes widened as he took in her labcoat and jeans. That was OK; he looked pretty different without his pinstripe on, too.

'Zander,' he said, thrusting his free hand forward. She took it on instinct; it was warm and strong and certain. Everything hers wasn't. 'Zander Rush. Station Manager for Radio EROS.'

Oh. That wasn't good.

He lifted his arm with something familiar and beige draped across it. 'You left your coat in the studio.'

The manager of one of London's top radio stations drove fifty kilometres to bring her a coat? No way.

'I considered that a small price to pay for getting the heck out of there,' she hedged. She hadn't really let herself think about the signed document on radio network letterhead sitting on her desk at home, but she was thinking about it now. And, she guessed, so was he.

The couple standing nearby suddenly twigged as to who she was. Their eyes lit up with recognition and the girl turned to the man and whispered.

Zander didn't miss it. 'Is there somewhere more private we can speak?'

'You have more to say?' It was worth a try.

His eyes shot around the room. 'I do. It won't take long.'

'This is a secure building. I can't take you inside. Let's walk.'

Conveniently, she had a coat. She shrugged into it and caught him as he was about to head back out through the giant open doors of the visitor centre.

'Back door,' she simply said.

Her ID opened the secure rear entrance and deposited them just a brisk walk from Bethlehem Wood. About as private as they were going to get out here on a Saturday. It got weekend traffic, too, but nothing like the rest of Wakehurst. Anyone else might have worried about setting off into a secluded wood with a stranger, but all Georgia could see was the strong, steady shape of his back as he'd sheltered her from prying eyes back in the elevator as her world imploded.

He wasn't here to hurt her.

'How did you find me?' she asked.

'Your work number was amongst the other contacts on our files. I called yesterday and realised where it was.'

'You were taking a chance, coming here on a Saturday.'

'I went to your apartment, first. You weren't there.'

So he drove all this way on a chance? He was certainly going to a lot of trouble to find her. 'A phone call wouldn't suffice?'

'I've left three messages.'

*Oh.*

'Yes, I...' What could she say that wouldn't sound pathetic? Nothing. 'I'm working my way up to my phone messages.'

He grunted. 'I figured the personal approach would serve me better.'

Maybe so; she was here, wasn't she? But her patience wasn't good at the best of times. 'What can I do for you, Mr Rush?'

'Zander.' He glanced at her sideways. Then, 'How are you doing, anyway?'

What a question. Rejected. Humiliated. Talked about by eight million strangers. 'I'm great. Never been better.'

His neat five o'clock shadow twisted with his lips. 'That's the spirit.'

Well, wasn't this nice? A walk in the forest with a total stranger, making small talk. Her feet pressed to a halt. 'I'm so sorry to be blunt, Mr Rush, but what do you want?'

He stopped and stared down at her, his eyes creasing. 'That's you being blunt?'

She shifted uncomfortably. But stayed silent. Silence was her friend.

'OK, let me get to the point…' He started off again. 'I'm here in an official capacity. There is a contract issue to discuss.'

She knew it.

'He said *no*, Mr Rush. That makes the contract rather hard to fulfil, don't you think? For both of us.' She hated how raw her voice sounded.

'I understand—'

'Do you? How many different ways do you hear your personal business being discussed each day? On social media, on the radio, on the bus, at the sandwich shop? I can't get away from it.'

'Have you thought about using it, rather than avoiding it?'

Was he serious? 'I don't want to use it.'

'You were happy enough to use it for an all-expenses-paid wedding.'

Of course that was what he thought. In some ways she'd prefer people thought she was doing it for the money. That was at least less pathetic than the truth. 'You're here for your pound of flesh—I get that. Why not just tell me what you want me to do?'

Not that she would automatically be saying yes. But it bought her time to think.

Grey eyes slid sideways as his gloveless hands slid into his pockets. 'I have a proposition for you. A way of addressing the contract. One that will be…mutually beneficial.'

'Does it involve a time machine so that I can go back a month and never sign the stupid thing?'

Never give in to her mother's pressure. Or her own desperate need for security.

His head dropped. 'No. It doesn't change the past. But it could change your future.'

She lifted her curiosity to him. 'What?'

He paused at an ornate timber bench and waited for her to sit. *Old-school gallantry.* Even Dan didn't do old school.

She sat. Curious.

'The media is hot for your story, Georgia. Your...situation has sparked something in them.'

'My rejection, you mean?'

He tilted his head. 'They'll be interested in everything you do. And if they're interested, then London will be interested. And if London is interested, then my network will want to exploit the existing contract however they can.'

Exploit? He was happy to use that word aloud? She tried not to let her surprise show.

'Georgia, under its terms they could still require you to come back for follow-up interviews.'

Her stomach crimped. 'To talk about how very much I'm not getting married? How I suddenly find myself alone with half my friends siding with my ex?' And the other half so determinedly *not* talking about it. 'Not exactly perky radio content.'

He shook his head. 'It's what they could ask. But I have a better idea. So that the benefit is not all one-way.'

She waited silently for his explanation. Mostly because she had no idea what to say.

'If you agree to seeing the year out, EROS is willing to redirect the funds from the engagement, wedding, and honeymoon to a different project. One that you might even enjoy.'

She frowned. 'What kind of project?'

He took a breath. 'Our listeners have connected with you—'

'You mean your listeners feel sorry for me.' Pity everywhere she looked.

'—and they want to see you bounce back from this disappointment. They want to follow you on your journey.'

She ignored that awful thought and glared at him. 'Really? You see into each of their hearts?'

His scoff vibrated through his whole body. 'We spend four million pounds a year on market research. We know how many sugars they each have in their coffee. Trust me. They want to know. You're like…them…to them.'

'And how is me working through my weekends in a lab going to make good radio? Because that's how I planned to get through this next year. Low profile and lots of work.'

'I'm asking you to flip that on its head. High profile and getting back out into the sunshine. Show them how you're bouncing back.'

Honesty made her ask in a tiny voice, 'What if I don't—bounce back? What then?'

Something flooded his eyes. Was it…compassion? 'We plan to keep you so busy you won't have time to wallow.'

*Wallow?* Anger rushed up and billowed under her coat. But she didn't let it out. Not directly. 'Busy with what?' she gritted.

'Makeovers. New clothes. Access to all the top clubs… You name it, we'll arrange it. EROS is making it our personal business to get you back on your feet. Total reinvention. And on your way to meeting Mr Right.'

She stared at him, aghast. 'Mr Right?'

'This is an opportunity to reinvent yourself and to find a new man to love.'

She just stared. There were no words.

It was only then he seemed to hesitate. 'I know it feels soon.' She blinked.

He frowned. Scowled. 'OK, I can see that you're not understanding—'

'I understand perfectly well. But I refuse. I have no interest in reinvention.' That wasn't entirely true—she'd often dreamed about the sorts of things she might have done if she'd grown up with money—but she certainly had no interest in a manufactured man-hunt.

'Why not?'

'Because there's nothing wrong with me, for a start.' *Hmm… defensive much?* 'I'm not in a hurry to have you tally up my apparently numerous deficiencies and broadcast them to the world.'

He stared at her. 'You're not deficient, Georgia. That's not the point of this.'

'Really? What is the point? Other than to tell women everywhere that being yourself is not sufficient to catch a good man.'

Something her gran had raised her never to believe. Something that was starting to look dangerously possible.

'OK, look… The point of this is ratings. That's all the network cares about. This promotion was mine and it went arse-up and so it's my mess to tidy. I just thought that we could spin it so that you can get something decent out of it. Something meaningful.' Sincerity blazed warm and intense from his eyes. 'This is an opportunity, Georgia. Fully paid. To do anything you want. For a year.'

She couldn't even be offended at having her life so summarily dismissed. *Arse-up* was a pretty apt description. She sighed. 'Why would you even care? I'm nobody to you.'

He glanced away. When he came back to her his eyes were carefully schooled. 'I feel a certain amount of responsibility. It was my promotion that ended your relationship. The least I can do is help you build a new one.'

'*I* ended my relationship,' she pressed. 'My decisions. I'm not looking to shift blame.'

'And so…?'

'I don't want to find someone to replace Dan. He wasn't just someone I picked up out of convenience.' Though, to her everlasting shame, she realised that maybe he was. And she'd almost made him her husband.

'So you're just going to hide out here for the next twelve months?'

*Yes.*

'No. I'm going to take a year off life to just get back to who I really am. To avoid men altogether and just remember what I liked about being by myself.' The idea blew across her mind like the leaves on the gravel path ahead of them. But it felt very right. 'It will be the year of Georgia.'

His eyes narrowed. 'The year of Georgia?'

'To please no one but me.' To find herself again. And see how she felt about herself when left alone in a room with no one else to fill the space.

'Well, then, think about how much you could do for yourself with a blank cheque behind you.'

It was a seductive image. All those things she'd always wanted to do—secretly—and never had the courage or the money to do. She could do them. At least some of them.

'What would you do,' he went on, sensing the shift in his fortune, 'if money was no object?'

*Build that time machine...* 'I don't know. Self-improvement, learn a language, swim the English Channel?'

That got his attention. 'The Channel, really?'

She shrugged. 'Well, I'd have to learn how to swim first...'

Suddenly he was laughing. 'The Year of Georgia. We could mix it up. Get a couple of experts to help us out with some ideas.' Grey eyes blazed into hers. 'Fifty thousand pounds, Georgia. All for you.'

She stared at him. For an age. 'Actually, I really just want all of this to go away. Can fifty grand buy that?'

The compassion returned. It flickered across his eyes and then disappeared. 'Not literally, but there's an extra-special level of feeding-frenzy that the public reserves for those not wanting the attention. Maybe fronting up to it will be a way to help end it?'

That made some sense. There was a seedy kind of fervour to the interest of the English public specifically because she and Dan were both trying so hard to avoid it. Maybe it tapped into the ancient predator parts of mankind, as if they were scenting a kill.

'You were willing to sell us your marriage before,' he summed up. 'Why not sell us your recovery? How is it different?'

'Sharing the happiest time of my life with the world would have been infinitely different.'

His eyes narrowed. 'Is that what you thought? That marrying him would make you happy?'

'Of course.' But then she stumbled. 'Happier. You know, *still* happy.'

It sounded lame even to her own ears.

'Clearly Bradford thought otherwise.' Then he took a breath. 'Why did you ask him if you weren't certain of his answer?'

Her brow folded. 'Because we'd been together for a year.'

'A year in which he thought you were both just enjoying each other's company.'

For a moment she'd forgotten—again—how very public her proposal was. And Dan's decline. Three million listeners had heard every excruciating word. She hid her shame by dropping her gaze to the path ahead of them.

'So...what? His twelve-month expiry date was approaching?'

She lifted her eyes again. 'It was your promotion, Mr Rush. "Give him a leap year nudge," you said in all your advertising.'

His eyes flicked away briefly. 'We didn't imagine anyone would take us literally.'

She stared at him as a small cluster of walkers passed by. Her friend's illness was none of his business. Nor was Kelly's eagerness to see a happy ever after for two people she loved. 'I misunderstood something someone close to him said,' she murmured.

Actually her mistake was in hearing what she wanted to hear. And letting her mother's expectations get to her. Her desperate desire to fill the void in her life with grandchildren. And then she'd awoken to EROS' promotion and decided it was some kind of sign.

And when she'd been shortlisted and then selected...well... Clearly it was meant to be.

And exactly *none* of those was even close to being a good excuse.

'I accept full responsibility for my mistake, Mr Rush—'

'Zander.'

'—and I'll need to seek some legal advice before answering you about the contract.'

'Of course.' He fished a business card from his pocket and handed it to her. 'You'd be foolish not to.'

Which was a polite, corporate way of suggesting she'd been pretty foolish already.

It was hard to argue.


'I think you should do it,' Kelly said, distracted enough that Georgia could well imagine her stirring a pot full of alphabet spaghetti in one hand, ironing a small school uniform with the other, and with the phone wedged between her ear and shoulder.

A normal day in her household.

'I thought for sure you'd tell me where he could stick his offer,' she said.

Kelly laughed. 'If not for those magic words...'

*Fifty thousand pounds.*

'You say magic words and I hear magic beans. I think this has the potential to grow into something really all-consuming.'

'So? Did you have any other plans for the next twelve months?'

The fact it was true—and that Kelly didn't mean to be unkind—didn't stop it hurting all the same. No, she had no particular plans that twelve months of fully paid *stuff* would interrupt. Which was a bit sad.

'George, listen. I don't want to bore you again with my life-is-for-the-living speech, but I would take this in a heartbeat if someone offered it to me.'

'Why? There's nothing wrong with you. You don't need reinvention.'

'There's nothing wrong with *you*. This doesn't have to be about that. This is an opportunity to do all the things you've put aside your whole life while you've been working and saving so hard. To live a little.'

'You know why I work as hard as I do.'

'I know. The whole "as God is my witness, I'll never be hungry again" thing. But you are not your mother, George. You are more financially secure than most people your age. Isn't there any room in your grand plan for some fun?'

She blinked, wounded both by Kelly's too-accurate summation of her entire life's purpose and by the implication of her words. 'I'm fun.'

Kelly's gentle laugh only scored deeper. 'Oh, love. No, you're not. You're amazing and smart and very interesting to be around, but you're about as much fun as Dan is. That's what made you two so—'

Kelly sucked her careless words back in. 'What I'm saying is, you have nothing to lose. Take this man's fifty grand and spoil yourself. Consider it a consolation prize for not getting to marry my stupid brother.'

'He's not stupid, Kel,' she whispered. 'He just doesn't love me.'

In the silence that followed, two little boys shrieked and carried on in the background. 'Well, I love you, George, and as your friend I'm telling you to take the money and run. You won't get a chance like this again.'

Kelly dragged her mouth away from the phone but not well enough to save Georgia's ears as she bellowed at one of her boys. 'Cal, enough!' She came back to their conversation. 'I'm going to have to go. World War Three is erupting. Let me know what you decide.'

Moments later, Georgia thumbed the disconnect button on her mobile and dropped it onto her plump sofa.

No surprises there, really. Of course Kelly would take the money. And the opportunity. She'd come so close to being robbed of life—and her boys of a mother—she was fully in marrow-sucking mode. And she was right—there really was nothing else going on in Georgia's life that a bunch of new activities would interrupt.

Her objections lay, not with the time commitment, but with the implication that she was broken. Deficient.

*About as much fun as Dan.* Did Kelly know what an indictment that really was? Mr Serious?

So that was three for three in favour. Kelly and her gran both thought it would be good for her and her mother…well, what else would a woman incapable of managing her money or her impulses say?

Which was part of the problem. Truth be told, Georgia had nothing against the idea of a bit of self-development of the social kind. She wanted to be a well-rounded person and maybe she had gone a bit too hard down the other path these past years. But the pitch of her mother's excited squeal was directly and strikingly proportional to her level of discomfort at the idea of frittering away fifty thousand perfectly good pounds—no matter how free—on meaningless, fluffy activity.

Her mother would have spent it in a week. Just as she spent every penny they ever had. They'd bounced through seven public houses before her gran called a halt and took a thirteen-year-old Georgia in with her.

And then it would be gone, with nothing to show for it but a fuller wardrobe, a liver in need of detox and a sleep debt the size of Wales.

She stretched out and pulled the well-thumbed EROS contract into her lap. It had her lawyer's recommendation paper-clipped to the front.

Sign, he said. And attached his invoice.

So that was four for four. Five if you counted the handsome and persuasive Zander Rush.

And only one against.

# CHAPTER THREE

*March*

Zander's assistant made an appointment right at the end of his day for her to sign the contract and so walking back into EROS was only *half* as intimidating as it might have been if it were full of staff.

An oblivious night-guard had just sat down at Reception instead of the two gossipy girls she'd met there the first time she visited, and most of the workstations in the communal area were closed down for the evening. Georgia clutched a printout of Zander's new contract in her hand and quietly trailed his assistant past the handful of people still beavering away at their desks. Most of them didn't raise their heads.

Maybe she was yesterday's news already.

Or maybe public interest had just swung around to Dan, instead, now that the calendar had flipped over to March. *Drop Dead Dan.* Apparently, he was fielding a heap of interest from the women's magazines and the tabloids, all determined to find him a match more acceptable than she. More worthy. London now thought he was too good for her. Not that *he'd* put it like that—or ever would have—but she could read between the lines. She didn't dare read the actual lines.

She shifted in her seat outside Zander's office.

Behind the frosted-glass doors, an elevated voice protested

strenuously. There was a low murmur where the shouted response should have been and then a final, higher-pitch burst.
Moments later one of the two doors flung open and a man
emerged—flushed, rushed—and stormed past her. He glanced
her way.

'A lamb to the bloody slaughter,' he murmured, a bit too
loud to have been accidental, before storming down the corridor and into one of the studios off to one side. She followed
his entire progress.

'Georgia.' A smooth voice dragged her focus back to the
doors.

She straightened, stood. Reached out her hand. The tiniest
of frowns crossed Zander's face before he enclosed her hand
in his and shook it. His fingers were as warm and lingering as
last time. And still pleasingly firm. 'I was beginning to think
we'd never see you again.'

'I had to think it over.' And over. Looking for any reasonable way out. And avoiding the whole thing, really.

'And?'

She sighed. 'And here I am.'

He stood back and signalled at his assistant, who was politely keeping her eyes averted, but not so much that she didn't
immediately decode and acknowledge his signal. Did that little finger-twiddle mean, *Hold my calls*? *Bring us coffee?* Or
maybe, *If she's not out in five minutes interrupt me with something fake but important.*

Perhaps the latter if the furrows above his brow were any
indication. He didn't look all that pleased to see her. So maybe
she really had taken too long with the contract.

'I needed to be sure I understood what you were asking.'
Ugh, way too defensive.

His eyes finally found hers and they didn't carry a hint of
judgement. 'And do you?'

She waved the sheaf of papers. 'All signed.'

A disproportional amount of relief washed across his face. He sat back in his expensive chair.

She tipped her head. 'You weren't expecting that?' She hated the thought that maybe there'd been more room for negotiation after all. She hated being played.

'I've learned never to try and anticipate the actions of people.' His eyes drifted to the door where the man had just stormed out.

'I had one question...'

The relief vanished and was replaced by speculation. 'Sure.'

'It's about the interviews. Is that really necessary? It seems very formal.'

'We just need an idea of who you are, so we know what we're starting with.'

'By filling out a questionnaire? I thought maybe if I had coffee with your assistant, told her a bit about myself—'

'Not Casey. She's not subjective enough.'

'Because she's a woman?'

'Because she's a card-carrying member of Team Georgia.'

Oh. How nice to have at least one person in her corner.

'Unless you were angling for a free lunch?'

She glared at him. 'Yes. Because all of this would be to-tally worth it if only I could get a free bowl of soup out of you.'

His scowl moderated into a half-smile.

'What about one of your other minions,' she tried.

His eyebrows shot up. 'Minions?'

'You have an assistant to do your bidding. And that man leaving just now didn't look like a man who enjoyed fair and equal status in his workplace.'

His frown deepened. 'I don't have minions. I do have staff.'

'Then any one of your staff.'

He studied her across the desk. 'No. Not one of my staff.'

She sighed. 'I'd really rather not do a questionnaire, Zan-der. It's too impersonal.' And a little bit insulting. As though a computer could tell her what was missing in her life when she was still struggling to work that out.

'Not one of my staff and not a form.'

'Then what?'

'Me.'

'You what?'

'I'll interview you.' He reached for a pen.

'N-now?' she stammered.

The half-smile graduated. 'No. I'm just making a couple of notes for Casey for tomorrow.'

She swivelled in her chair. 'She's gone?'

'Yes. Why?'

'I thought you... Didn't you signal for her to do something for you just now?'

'Yes, I told her to go home. Just because I keep long hours doesn't mean she has to. She's got a young family to get home to.'

So they were...alone? Why on earth did that make her pulse spike? Just once. She'd walked in a secluded wood with him. Being alone in an office wasn't all that scandalous. Except that it was *his* office, full of *his* comfy, oversized furniture and all of a sudden she felt a lot like an outclassed Goldilocks.

She pushed half out of her chair. 'I should go.'

'What about the interview? I thought we could go and grab a drink, talk. I can get what I need.'

For a bright woman, an astonishing amount of nothing filled her head just then. He prowled to the front of his desk and stood by her chair so that she had no choice but to stand and let him shepherd her out of his office.

'The contract...' she breathed.

He relieved her of the pages, flicked to the back one and signed it, unread. She pressed her lips together. 'I should have gifted myself a luxury car in small print.'

His lips parted, revealing smooth, white, even teeth. 'Where would you drive a luxury car?'

'You never know. Maybe that's something I'd like to get experience with—I've never driven anything flashier than a Vauxhall.'

His eyes softened as they alighted on her. Then he reached deep into his trouser pocket and tossed her a bundle of keys. They were still warm from his body heat. Toasty warm. She lifted her eyes to his.

'Never too early to get started. Consider this the first Year of Georgia activity. Driving a luxury car.'

'Not your Jag?' she gasped.

'Not flashy enough for you?'

Excitement tangled with dread. 'What if I scratch it? Or dent it?' Or drive it into the Thames in her excitement?

'You strike me as a careful driver.'

He ushered her out of the door, keys still lying limp and unwelcome on her palm. She closed her fingers around them.

'Besides,' he said, 'I have outstanding insurance.'

*Why would you even care?*

Her words had haunted him ever since she'd uttered them, wide-eyed and confused, when he'd first hit her with his counter-proposal. He did care—very much—on a personal level that even he barely understood, so he'd been shoving the echo of her words way down deep every time it bubbled to the surface.

Rod and Nigel were already celebrating a ratings coup— even bad PR was good PR in the communications industry— but they'd left the details of what the coming year would entail up to him. As long as Zander got her on board, that was all they cared about. Locking down the contract and making the best use of the publicity windfall.

This desperate attempt to make sure she got something back for her troubles, that was all him. It just didn't seem right to screw a girl at the most vulnerable moment of her life.

And he knew all about that moment. He'd lived it. He knew how it shaped his life.

It was stupid; he could hardly say that he'd bonded with Georgia the moment he decided to shield her from the prying eyes waiting in Reception. Back in the elevator. But he had. She'd lingered somewhere in the back of his mind from the moment she'd fallen so gratefully on the gesture, and then she'd popped up, unsolicited, when he wasn't armed.

In the middle of important meetings.

Late at night.

Out on the roads as he thudded one foot in front of the other.

'You seem to be dealing with this quite well,' he murmured as the waiter topped up both their glasses in his favourite Hampstead bar. 'Given how you felt about the whole idea last time we met.'

She took a long, steady breath. 'It seems I'm the only one of a longish list of people who doesn't think there's room for improvement with Georgia Version-Two.'

'Give yourself some credit,' he murmured, saluting her with his glass before taking a sip. 'You're more together than you think.'

'Based on what?'

'My observations.'

'During one quick walk in the woods?'

'I'm paid to pay attention to first impressions.'

Her eyes narrowed. 'The elevator?'

'That was a tough few minutes for you and you handled them well.'

She snorted. 'Weeping while your back was turned?'

He smiled. 'How someone reacts under extreme pressure tells you a lot about them. You were unfailingly courteous even as you were dying inside.'

Uncertainty flooded her dark eyes. 'You saw that?'

'But you didn't let it have you. You stayed in control.'

'You didn't see what happened to me once I got home,' she murmured.

He chuckled. 'I said you were strong, not a machine.'

He glanced down to her twisting fingers. Elegant, sensibly manicured hands. He wondered how much else Georgia Stone was sensible about. And what secret things she wasn't.

And he shut that curiosity down as fast as it came.

'So. Have you given any thought to the kinds of things you might like to do with the Year of Georgia?'

'No.'

A lie, for sure. She was human. Who wouldn't start thinking about how to spend that kind of money?

'Top restaurants? Boats? A-list parties? A taste of how the other half live.'

She shrugged. 'I can see how they live. It doesn't interest me, particularly.'

'Why not?'

'Because it's…frivolous.'

*Wow.* 'That's rather judgemental, don't you think?'

She leaned forward. 'More cars than one person can drive and glamorous houses and wardrobes bulging with unworn clothes?'

'Where'd you get that impression? Television?' She frowned. 'I have more cars than I can drive at once. A nice house and enough suits for two weeks without laundering.' As he knew from experience. 'But I wouldn't call myself frivolous. Maybe there's more to it than you imagine.'

And he wouldn't flatter himself that this was about him. This was an older prejudice at work.

She dropped her eyes briefly. 'Perhaps. But I'm still not interested enough to try. I like my own world.'

'Science and beautiful gardens? What else?'

She stared him down. 'Classical music. Rowing. Old movies. History.'

He blew out a breath. One part of him sighed at the image

of a life filled with those things. Quiet, solitary, gentle things. But the station manager in him baulked. 'Getting our listeners excited about rowing and classical music is going to be a hard sell.' Along with the rest.

She sat up straighter. 'Not my problem.'

The first real emotion she'd shown him. Shame it was offence. 'It kind of is, Georgia. You have a signed contract to honour. We need to find a way forward in this.'

Her astute eyes pinned him. 'As long as it also works for your listeners?'

'There must be things that they'll enjoy that you will, too.'

She stared at him. 'I won't do it if it's portrayed as me trying to find a man. Or to improve myself enough to find one.'

'Just the Year of Georgia, then. The Valentine's Girl getting back on her feet. You really cared for Daniel, our listeners will buy that.' God… Could he hear himself? He sounded just like Rod. Always an angle. Always a carrot. 'We'll assign someone from the station to—'

'No. I don't want one of them with me.'

'One of who?'

'One of the people who were there for the proposal. I don't want them coming with me.'

She didn't trust them. And he understood why. Though what she didn't understand was that the whole sodding mess was *his* fault. Not theirs.

'OK, I'll hire someone esp—'

'No strangers, either.' Her face pinched in several places.

'Georgia, if I can't use one of my team and I can't hire someone, who am I going to get to do it?'

'You do it. I know you.'

His laugh was as loud as it was immediate. 'Do you know what I get paid an hour?'

'Too much to actually get paid by the hour, I'm sure. But that is my condition.' She did her best to look adamant. Even that was moderated by a faintly apologetic sheen to her steady gaze. 'Take it or leave it.'

She had no idea how to negotiate. The innocence was insanely refreshing. 'You've already signed the contract,' he pointed out gently.

But even as the words came out of his mouth his brain ticked over, furiously. His assistant would jump at the chance for some extra responsibility, so he could offload some lower-end tasks to Casey. And if this was what it would take to get Georgia fully on board...

But he held his assent back, in case it had more power a few moments later.

His entire life was about holding things back until they had the most advantage.

'My days are packed out from dawn until dusk.'

Georgia shrugged. 'I have a job, too, so they're going to be evening and weekend things anyway, I imagine.'

It was hard not to admire her for sticking to her guns. Not too many people made a habit of saying no to him these days. He had them all too scared.

'I have things I like to do on my weekends,' he argued. But not very convincingly. Hard-to-get was all part of the game.

One dark, well-shaped eyebrow lifted. 'How badly do you want these ratings?'

A stain of colour came to her cheeks. Either she was shocked at her own audacity or she was enjoying giving him some stick. He used the time she thought he was thinking about her offer to study her features instead. She had a right-hand-side dimple that totally belied the determination of those set lips, and she had a chin built for protesting.

That was probably long enough. He hissed as if he hadn't made his decision sixty seconds ago. 'Fine. I'll do it.'

Her triumph was so brief. It only took her a heartbeat to realise that his commitment had fully sealed hers. And her next twelve months.

'One more condition,' she hurried as a pair of drink menus arrived. It was his turn to lift a brow. 'No one mentions Dan. No one. You will leave him completely alone.'

Loyalty blazed from her chocolate eyes.

Somewhere down deep where constancy used to live in him, he admired her for continuing to protect the man she'd injured. A man she still cared for even though he'd also hurt her horribly. It said she might have been impetuous and naïve but she was faithful. And that was a rare commodity in his world. Her hurt and anger were very clearly directed at herself. In fact, the most notable thing about her manner was the absence of the flat, lifeless lack of interest that he associated so closely with heartbreak—and knew so intimately.

He wondered if she'd even realised yet that her heart wasn't broken.

'OK, Daniel is out of it.'

'And get the media to lay off him.'

He snorted. Whoever taught Georgia about manners forgot to teach her about pushing her luck. 'No one can halt that train now that it's moving, Georgia. I can promise EROS won't use him, but there's nothing I can do about him being London's most wanted. He's a big boy. He'll be fine.'

Besides, judging by what he heard on the broadcast, Daniel Bradford could look after himself.

He leaned forward and locked his eyes on hers. 'You've played this well—' *for a civilian* '—but I've bent about as far as I'm going to go. I'll have an amendment to the contract drawn up and ready for your signature next week.'

She nodded and sank back in her side of the booth.

'How about some dinner?'

She just blinked at him.

'You do eat dinner?'

'Um, yes. Though not usually out. Except for special occasions.'

She truly hadn't begun to imagine ways of spending her

huge windfall? He tried one last time to prove that she was like everyone else. 'Don't tell me you're another mad-keen home chef?'

Her laugh was automatic. 'No, definitely not.'

'You don't cook?'

'I prepare food. But it's not really cooking. The latest in a number of reasons it was probably just as well Dan declined my proposal.'

She certainly was taking her failed marriage-bid a hell of a lot better than he'd taken his. Did that say more about her or Bradford?

Or him?

He fired up his tablet and tapped a few keys. 'I think we just found your first official Year of Georgia idea.'

'Eating out in every restaurant in London?'

'Culinary school.' He chuckled.

She stared. 'I hated home economics at school. What makes you think I'll enjoy it now?'

'Half the women on my staff are right into those social cooking classes. Wine, conversation, cooking techniques from the experts. The sessions must have something going for them.'

Her lips tightened. 'I'm not sure I'd want to go where your staff—'

'God, no.' He pushed his chair back and stood. 'That's the last thing I want, too.'

'You?'

'I'll be coming along. Or have you changed your mind?'

Her delicate brows folded closer together. 'It's not me doing it for me if I'm doing it with you. The dynamic would be all wrong.'

Dynamic. That sounded almost credible. What was she really worried about?

'I need to be there to record your progress, but...you have a point. We'll do it together, but separate. Like we don't know each other. I'll just shadow you. Watch.'

A streak of colour ran up her jaw. 'Won't that be weird?'

He pushed his glass away and leaned in closer. 'Georgia, I'm going to have a solution for any hurdle you put up. You've signed the contract. How about working with me on this instead of against?'

She sighed. Stared at him with those unreadable eyes. 'OK. Sorry.' She took a sip of white wine. 'What did you have in mind?'

'That's a long list.' Georgia stretched and read the upside-down sheet in front of Zander.

'A year is a long time. But we don't have to go with all of these. Plus things might come up along the way so we need to leave room for those. If you had to shortlist, which ones would you enjoy the most?'

He spun the paper around to her and passed her his fancy pen. She asterisked Wimbledon, cooking classes—which she agreed to because he'd indicated his listeners would love it, not because she actually wanted to know the difference between flambé and sauté—cocktail-making class, truffle-making, and a makeover. That last one because she got the sense he really thought it was important. She tugged her sensible shirt down further over her sensible trousers.

'I really want to do this one.' She circled one down near the bottom, taking a risk. It wasn't what he'd be expecting at all. And unlike some of the others this one actually did interest and intrigue her.

'Ice carving?'

'How amazing would that be? Ooh, and this one...' Another asterisk.

'Spy school?'

She lifted excited eyes. 'Can you imagine?'

He shook his head. 'I don't need to imagine. I'm going to find out.'

She sipped her wine.

'What about travel?' he asked.

'What about it?'

'Not interested in the thought of a holiday?'

Flying to a whole other country seemed a lot to ask. Besides, she didn't have a passport. Just the idea of applying for one got her blood thrumming.

'Where could I go?' she breathed.

His smile was almost indulgent. If it weren't also so confused. Had he never met anyone whose gratification went so far beyond delayed it was non-existent?

'Anywhere you want,' he said.

As she holidayed in her apartment as a rule, anything further afield than Brighton just didn't occur to her. 'Where would be good for your listeners?'

Zander shrugged. 'New York? Ibiza?'

Her breath caught... *Ankara?* She'd wanted to go to Turkey since seeing a documentary on its ancient history.

But no, that seemed too much. Fanciful. She wrote down *Ibiza* on the bottom of the list. That seemed like the kind of place EROS listeners would like to hear about. The party capital of Europe. Fast-pour bars and twenty-four-hour clubs and duelling dance arenas and swollen feet and ringing ears.

Oh, yay.

'I might add some things, as we go along. Things that occur to me.' Things she'd like to do but didn't want Zander knowing about. Though of course they wouldn't stay secret for long.

'That's fine. Just hook them up with Casey. I'll just go where she sends me.'

'That's very accommodating of you. Compliance won't do much for your reputation as a fearsome boss,' she said.

One eye twitched. 'I'm not fearsome; I just want them to think that I am.'

'Why?' That was no way to enjoy your work.

'Because it gets things done. I'm not there to be their friend.'

She thought of her own boss. A whacky, brilliant man whom

she absolutely adored. 'You don't think people would work just as hard with respect and admiration as their motivation?'

He lifted his gaze. 'I'd like to think they respect me. I just don't need them to like me.'

Or want them to? Something in his demeanour whispered that. But there wasn't much else she could say about that without offending him. Besides, last time she checked he was the most successful person she knew. And she didn't know him at all.

Silence fell. 'What do you do on your weekends?' she finally asked.

'What?'

'You said you had things to do on your weekend. What kinds of things?'

He regarded her steadily. 'Weekend stuff.'

She lifted both her eyebrows.

'I train.' He frowned.

*Lord. Blood from a stone!* 'For...?'

'For events.'

She took a stab. 'Showjumping? Clay shooting? Oh!' She drained the last of her wine. 'Ice dancing.'

A reluctant smile crept onto his face. 'Endurance running. I compete in marathons.'

'Truly?'

He chuckled. 'Yes.'

'What sort of distances?'

'Forty or fifty kilometres. It depends.'

'A *weekend*?' Her half-shriek drew glances from around the noisy bar.

His lips twisted. 'A day.'

*A day!* 'Well, that explains the body—'

Horror sucked the words back in, but not fast enough. *Oh, God!* She quietly pushed her nearly empty glass far away from her.

'I have to keep my fitness up, so I run every morning and I do long runs or hikes every weekend.'

'Every weekend?'

'Pretty much.'

Wow. 'Just running. For hours on end?'

'Or hard hiking. That's why it's called endurance.'

'Sounds lonely.' But also kind of…zen. Kind of what she did when she wandered deep into the dark heart of forests.

'I don't mind the solitude,' he murmured.

'Is that why you do it?'

His answer was fast. As if he'd defended himself on that point often. 'I do it for the challenge. Because I can. And I do my best thinking out there.'

Fifty kilometres. That was a lot of thinking time.

'Just…wow. I'm impressed.'

'Don't get too excited. In competition we can do that in under four hours.'

Georgia shook her head. 'Put marathon running on the list.'

He looked up sharply. 'You want to run a marathon?'

'God, no. I have two left feet. But I've never seen one. I can just watch you. Help you train.'

Intense discomfort flooded his face.

Once again she'd managed to misread a man. This wasn't a friendship. They weren't bonding. This was a business arrangement with the sole purpose of tracking *her* activity. Why on earth would he want her around during his private time? He probably had a raft of friends actually of his choosing to hang out with—and many of them women.

'I…uh…'

She'd stuffed up big enough to actually make a man stammer. World class.

'You know what?' she breezed, not feeling the slightest bit breezy. 'I've changed my mind. Me watching you run would make *terrible* radio. Scratch that off the list.' Was she a convincing liar? They'd find out. His pen was still frozen over the page and so there was nothing to scratch out, so she said the only other thing that came into her head.

'Another drink?'

The list grew as long as the evening. They hit the Internet for ideas of cool things for her to do in London. Pretty soon they had learn-to-dance classes, movie premieres, and a royal polo match.

'Aquasphering!' she said, a little bit too loud. 'Whatever that is.'

'Really? That's your kind of thing?'

'None of it is my thing—isn't that the point? Pushing myself out of my comfort zone.' *Wa-a-ay* out of it.

'Can we afford a seat on a commercial spaceflight?' she blurted, tapping the tablet's glossy screen. 'That would be exciting.'

He smiled. 'No. We can't. And we don't really have the time for it to become more mainstream.'

'Pff. You suck.'

Zander stared at her. Assessing. 'I think I need to get some food into you.'

'I told you I didn't do this for the soup.'

'I was thinking of something a little more solid than soup.'

Judgement stung, low and sharp. She sat up straighter. 'I'm not drunk.'

'No, you're not. But you will be if you keep going like this.'

'Maybe the new me drinks more often.'

He gathered up their papers and his tablet and returned them to his briefcase. 'Really? This is how you want to start the Year of Georgia? By getting hammered?'

She stared at him. Thought about that. 'Have we started?'

'First day.'

'Then we should leave.' Because, no, she didn't want to start that way.

'Let me feed you. I have somewhere in mind. We can walk. Clear your head.'

'Why isn't your head fuzzy? You've been matching me drink for drink.'

He shrugged. 'Body mass?'

She relaxed back into the booth and smiled happily. 'That's so unfair.' Then she sat bolt upright again, her fingers reaching for her phone before her mind was even engaged. 'I should ring Dan. I need to explain.'

Zander caught her hand before it could do more than curl around her phone. 'No. Let's not do that on an empty stomach. Let's go get some food.'

He was right. She needed to talk to Dan face to face, not over the phone. She stood. 'OK. What are we having?'

'We could start your cooking lesson tonight. Something informal.'

'I live miles from here.'

He smiled. 'I don't.'

And just like that—*bam!*—she was sober. Zander Rush was taking her back to his place. To feed her. To teach her to make food. Something about that seemed so...intimate.

'You know what?' she lied. 'I have some things to do tonight before work tomorrow. I think maybe I should just head home.'

'What about food?'

If she was clear-headed enough to lie she was clear-headed enough to catch the tube. 'We're one block from the station.'

His smile grew indulgent. 'I know. You drove us here.'

'It's on the same line as Kew Gardens. I used to catch it home all the time.' So she knew it well.

'At least let me walk you to the station, then.'

She shot to her feet. 'That would be lovely, thank you.'

He shook his head. 'Still so courteous.'

She shrugged. 'Old-school upbringing.'

'Traditional parents?'

Her laugh was more of a bark. 'Definitely not. My gran

raised me mostly. To give me some stability. My mother really wasn't…well adapted…to parenting.'

He threw her a sideways look. 'I'm the youngest of six to older parents so maybe we were raised by a similar generation?'

It took just a few minutes to walk down to the station and something in her speech or her steady forward movement or her riveting, non-stop chatter about her childhood must have convinced him she was fine to be left alone because he didn't try and stop her again.

He paused by the white entry gate. 'Well…'

'You'll be in touch?'

'Casey will. My assistant.'

Of course. He had minions.

'She'll pull together a schedule for the next few months, to get us started.'

'So…I guess I'll see you at the first one, then.'

'Remember, we'll be strangers as far as anyone else is concerned. I'm just your shadow. I won't even acknowledge you when I arrive.'

Weird. But better. If they were doing these things together she'd just get too comfortable. And that wasn't a good idea, judging by how comfortable she'd been for the past few hours. 'I'll remember. See you then.'

She stepped towards the ticket gate, then turned back and smiled. 'Thanks for letting me drive the Jag.'

'Any time.'

Georgia waved again and then disappeared into the station. Zander turned and jogged across the pedestrian crossing, then ducked down the commercial lane that led to the back of the garden of his nearby house where they'd parked the Jag. Except she thought they just got lucky with a street park convenient to his favourite bar, not parking in front of his house.

He was really out of practice. Who took a woman to a bar, then drank so that he couldn't drive her home? Who let a woman ride the tube alone at night?

A man who was trying really hard not to feel as if he was on a date, that was who.

He'd first caught himself back at his office when she'd thrust her hand out so professionally and he'd felt a stab of disappointment. What did he expect, a kiss on each cheek? Of course she was all business. This was…business.

And this was just an after-hours work meeting. He'd almost sabotaged himself by inviting her back to his house to eat, but it had just tumbled from his lips. The old Zander never would have let so many hours pass without taking care to make sure they'd both eaten. It had been a long time since the new Zander came along. This Zander had perfectly defined business muscle but it had come at the expense of social niceties.

Any muscle would atrophy without use.

And then the coup de grâce. *Any time.* He could have said 'you're welcome' or 'think nothing of it' but he went with 'any time'. As though there'd be a repeat performance.

He pushed through the gate to his property and started down the long, winding path between the extensive gardens to the conservatory.

Clearly something of the old him still existed. Something that responded to Georgia's easy company and complete failure to engage with him the way others did. She just didn't care who he was or that he was the only thing standing between her and a lawsuit. Or maybe she just didn't recognise it.

She stared up at him with those big brown eyes and treated him exactly like everyone else.

No one did that any more. Even Casey—the closest thing he had to a friend at work—was always super careful never to cross a line, to always stop just short of the point where familiarity became contempt. Even she was sensitive to how much of her future rested in his hands.

Because he was so thorough in reminding them all. Regularly.

His minions.

He smiled. The irony was he didn't think that way at all. Not deep down. He believed in the power of teams and much preferred collaborative working groups to the way he did things now. They'd served him well back in the day when every programme he'd produced had been the product of a handful of hard-working people. But there was no getting around the fact that EROS really did run better with a clear, controlled gulf between himself and the people who worked for him. And he didn't mind the gulf; it meant no complications between friendships and workplace relationships.

And driving Georgia home would have been a complication.

Having her here, in his house, would have been a complication.

He had a signed contract; the time for courting The Valentine's Girl, professionally, was over. He should have just given her a list of activities that the station was prepared to send her to and been done with it. Instead of being a sap. Instead of reacting to an event fifteen years old and letting it colour his better judgement.

Instead of empathising.

Just because he'd been exactly where Georgia was; on the arse-end of a declined proposal. Only in his case, he got all the way down the aisle before realising his fiancée wasn't coming down behind him because she was on her way to Heathrow with her supportive bridesmaids. What followed was a horrible half-hour of shouting and recriminations before the priest managed to clear the church. Lara's family and friends all went wildly on the defensive—as you would if it was someone *you* loved that had done something so shocking. His side of the church rallied around him so stoically, which only inflamed Lara's family more because they knew—*knew*—that there were a hundred better ways to not proceed with a marriage than just not turning up. Less destructive ways. But she'd gone with the one that would cause her the least pain.

And, chump that he was, he actually preferred that. He

wasn't in the business of wishing pain on people he loved back then.

The heartbreak was bad enough, slumped in the front row of the rioting church, but he'd had to endure the public humiliation in front of everyone he cared about. Their whispers. Their pity. Their side-taking. Worse, their determined, well-meant support. Every bit as excruciating and public as Georgia's turn-down live on air. Just more contained.

Like atomic fusion.

But the after-effects rippled out for a decade and a half.

He jogged up the stairs and headed straight for his study. The most important room in his house. The work he got done there was the difference between just-hanging-on in the network and excelling. No one excelled on forty hours a week. He was putting in eighty, easy.

It was the one thing he could thank Lara for.

Setting him up for the kind of success that gave him a luxurious study in a big house in Hampstead Heath and had him rubbing shoulders with some of the most powerful people in the country.

And just like that he was thinking of Georgia again. Her crack about big houses and unworn clothes and crowded garages. There was a reason he parked the Jag on the street. Because both the cars in his garage were worth more. He liked his life. Excessive though it might be at times. He barely drove the Lotus or the Phantom but he could if he wanted to. And he could look at them whenever he wanted. But they represented something to him. As did the suits and the house and the title on his business card.

They represented the fact that no one would ever pity him again.

And, God help him, no one would ever come to his emotional aid as they'd had to in that church. Not family. Not friends. He would never allow himself to be in that kind of vulnerable position twice.

Money made sure of that.

Success made sure of that.

The corporate world might be a brutal mistress but it was constant. And if you were going to get screwed you'd always see it coming.

He'd never be hijacked again.

How pathetic that she needed a good excuse to go to Kew and *accidentally* see Dan. If she'd found the courage to face the truth about her reasons for proposing, could she really not face Dan himself? The man who'd been such an important and steady part of her life for the past year. Even longer if you counted their friendship before that.

She did need to speak to him face to face. Six weeks was long enough to take the sting out of everything for both of them.

And she had seeds to deliver to his colleagues for identification.

She dropped them to the propagation department and then hit the pathways across Kew to the behind-the-scenes greenhouses. That was where Dan spent most of his time—cultivating the carnivores, he called it—as popular with him as they were with the public.

She knew these paths like the freckles on her body. Long before she knew Dan.

*Huh. Look at that. Life before Dan.* She'd almost forgotten what that felt like.

Determined not to cut corners—even turf deserved not to be trampled—she followed the path the long way around to the plain glasshouse where Dan primarily worked. Her pulse began to thump.

As she approached it the doors opened and a woman emerged.

'Oh, excuse me!' Georgia exclaimed, her hand to her chest. She had crazy blonde curls, and the serviceable work-coats that everyone wore here. But she had a tight pink dress beneath it, bright, manicured nails, three inch heels and flawless make-up.

*Not* like everyone else here.

'Nearly got you.' The woman smiled, stepping back to hold the door.

That was perfect, too. Her eyes dropped briefly to the woman's ID tag and, just like that, all Georgia's carefully constructed excuses about why she didn't have better clothes and better hair vanished in a puff of perfume. This woman was an orchid specialist—she worked with dirt all day. Yet she could do that and still look like this.

What excuse did she herself have?

'Can I help you?' the woman said.

'I'm looking for Daniel Bradford.'

'He's out in the display house tending to a struggling *Nepenthes tentaculata*. Can I give him a message?' The slightest hint of curiosity filled her eyes.

It was pure luck that she hadn't run into someone she knew, someone much more familiar with the past relationship between she and Daniel. She wasn't going to blow the opportunity for anonymity.

'No, I know the way. I'll chase him down there. Thank you.' Georgia stepped back from the entrance.

The woman stepped away from the doors, smiling, and they swung shut behind her. 'You're welcome.'

She turned left, Georgia turned right. But she watched the woman walk away from her. Heels. They did something very special to a walk, even on gravel and grass. Pity she didn't have a single pair above a serviceable inch.

Maybe that was something she could put on her Year of Georgia list.

*Learn to walk in heels.*

And not because men liked them—though the distracted glances of two groundsmen passing the woman confirmed that they did—but because heels were a side of herself that she just never indulged.

Heels and pole dancing. They could go on the side-list she was quietly developing.

Though both could easily break her neck.

It took nearly ten minutes to cross out into the public area and work her way around to the carnivorous-plants exhibit. The doors were perpetually closed to keep the ambient temperature inside right but, unlike the clunky ones behind the scenes, these opened and closed whisper quiet.

She took a breath. 'Dan?'

The silence stayed silent, but somehow it changed. Grew loaded. And Georgia knew she'd been heard.

'I know you're here, Dan.'

'Hey.' He stepped out from behind a large sign. Confused. Wary. 'I didn't know you were coming.'

'I was dropping down some stock for identification. Thought I'd come and say hi.'

Oh, so horribly bright and false.

He nodded. 'Hi.'

Silence. Maybe six weeks weren't enough. 'How are you doing?' she risked.

'OK. Managing.'

The intense scrutiny. Right. 'It's not getting better?'

His lips thinned. 'Not really.'

She nodded. More silence. 'So…I've come to say I'm sorry. Again.'

'Your emails and messages not enough?'

'I didn't want… Not without at least seeing you.' God. How could it be this hard breaking up with someone when you were already broken up?

He shrugged. 'Fodder for the paparazzi.'

She spun around, expecting to see flashes of cameras behind her. 'Oh, God, I didn't even think of that…'

'That's starting to sound familiar.'

The unkind words cut but she knew they were more than deserved. And short of ratting out Kelly to her brother, she couldn't enlighten him otherwise. She sighed. 'Look, Dan, if I could undo it I would. I know you didn't ask for any of this.'

'Done is done.'

Well… 'Not quite, actually.'

His shaggy head tipped. But his hazel eyes darkened with warning. 'Georgia…'

'I'm… I signed a contract with the radio station, for the whole…' She couldn't even use the word *proposal*. 'I have to see it through.'

'I hope you mean "I" and not "we".'

'Not we. I made it a condition that you weren't involved at all.' Something she should have thought about originally, perhaps. 'It's not about us, it's about me. Me getting myself all fixed up.'

God love him, he frowned. 'You weren't broken, George. It was just a really stupid thing to have done.'

'I know. But for me that's symptomatic of being broken. I don't do stupid things. I'm supposed to be rock-solid and reliable and never-changing like you.' It was why she'd allowed herself to think they might make a life together at all.

His scowl deepened.

*Say what you have to say and get out.* 'So I really just wanted to make sure you were OK and to tell you why you'll be hearing more from me on the station.'

'Are you kidding?' He snorted. 'I'll never listen to them again.'

Oh, right.

'You realise it will just stir things up again every time you go on there?' he huffed.

'Zander thinks that it will help draw attention away from you. Keep it on me.' Where it belonged.

'Zander?'

'He's the station manager. It was his promotion.'

The scowl returned. 'Forgive me if I don't put a lot of faith in the opinion of anyone who would think up a promotion like that.'

The intense desire to defend Zander burbled up out of no-where. 'This is my responsibility, Dan. I'm trying to fix it as best I can.'

His brilliant mind ticked over behind carefully shielded eyes. 'I know. Sorry. You do whatever you need to, George.' He took a breath. 'And I'll do whatever I need to, to stay out of it.'

Intriguingly cryptic but fair enough. 'OK.'

They both shuffled awkwardly. 'So…I'll let you get back to your sick pitcher plant.'

His eyes narrowed. 'How did you know what I'm working on?'

'One of your colleagues told me.' And for no good reason at all she expanded. 'Blonde hair, flashy dresser.'

*Cripes, Georgia, you might as well just ask him outright. 'Why wasn't I good enough for you?'*

His eyes grew even more guarded. 'Right. Yes, she's new.'

'Pretty.' Pretty different from everyone round here, that was. Because actually she was gorgeous.

He shrugged. 'I guess.'

OK, he wasn't going to play. She should have known. 'Well, I should get going.' It hit her then that she would quite possibly never see him again. She frowned. 'I don't quite know how to say goodbye to you for the last time ever. It feels really wrong.'

But that was all, she realised. Just intensely awkward. It didn't really hurt.

*Huh.*

He walked forward, wiped the earth from his hand and then took hers. 'Bye, George. Don't be too hard on yourself. No one died, here.'

No. Except the part of her that used to be happy with herself. She squeezed his fingers. 'Take care, Dan.'

'Maybe I'll see you round.'

She turned. Left. And then it was done. That entire chapter of her life closed as silently and gently as the hydraulic doors of the greenhouse.

And still, no hurt. Just sadness. Like losing a good friend.

Did Dan feel the same? Was that why he'd never wanted their relationship to be more? His sister had always hinted at something big in his past, but he'd never shared and she'd never felt she could ask. Kind of symptomatic of why they weren't right for each other, really. He didn't want more because he didn't have more in him to give. And maybe neither did she. How long might they have gone on like that if she hadn't brought their non-relationship to a startling and public end?

She'd had no trouble at all imagining herself as Mrs Bradford, obligatory kids hanging off her skirts. As if it were just the natural extension of the life they'd had. She enjoyed his conversation, she liked to share activities with him, the sex was as good as she figured she would ever get. He was bomb-proof and reliable and she'd been drawn to the qualities in him that screamed *stability*. Because she'd had so little of it in her past. But she'd never gone breathless waiting to walk into Dan's office. She'd never felt as cherished with him as she had standing behind a perfect stranger in an elevator as he protected her from prying eyes.

Zander.

About as unsuitable for her as any man could be, yet he'd stirred more emotion in her in a few meetings than had the man she'd been planning on marrying.

All outstanding reasons to keep her distance, emotionally.

This was the Year of Georgia. Not the year of panting after sexy, rich, unavailable men. She'd made enough bad decisions in the interests of what her friends or the rest of the world was doing; she needed to have a good look inside and see what *she* wanted to do.

Even if she was a bit scared that she'd look deep inside and find nothing left.

# CHAPTER FOUR

*April*

THE buzz in the perfume-rich room hushed but intensified as Zander walked into it. Georgia saw him from the corner of her eye but made a concerted effort *not* to see him. Every other woman in the place did the same but for totally different reasons.

'*Dieu merci!* The testosterone balance in the room just doubled,' the male chef joked and drew even more anti-attention to Zander's arrival. He smiled thinly.

Georgia had quickly realised that attending alone was a mistake. Every other woman there was paired up with a girlfriend, so, quite apart from whether there were any men in the room, she felt like a failure already. Learning to love doing things solo was going to be a much bigger challenge than just growing accustomed to doing things without a man by her side. Hard enough to be doing things that weren't in her comfort zone, but to be doing them alone...

Effectively alone. Her eyes snuck to Zander again, briefly.

'*Alors.*' Chef clapped his chopping board onto the bench top a few times to call the unruly crowd to order. 'Places.'

What did that mean? Her first reaction was to watch Zander but if he was any wiser he wasn't giving anything away, so she took her cues from the other participants instead. They each dragged a tall stool along one edge of the oversized kitchen bench as Chef laid out a generous wine glass in front of each place from the other side. Two women practically turned an ankle vying for the spot closest to Zander who—wisely—took up the seat right at the end so that he only had to negotiate one interested feminine neighbour.

Georgia waited until last and found herself in the space furthest from him. She filled her glass with water before anyone could put anything more ill-advised in it from the rapidly emptying bottle of chardonnay doing the rounds.

Getting tipsy in front of Zander once was bad enough.

'First point of the evening to the woman down the end. What's your name, *petite fleur*?'

All eyes snapped her way, including Zander's.

Every awful moment of her school career came rushing back with the unexpected attention. It never paid to be the brightest—and poorest—at secondary school. It led to all kinds of unwanted attention. 'Georgia.'

'Well, Miss Georgia,' Chef improvised in ever-thickening French, 'while wine is *perfection* for enjoying the consumption of a meal, water is, without question, the best choice for preparing one. Until you know what you're doing, of course. You want your tastebuds unassailed. You want your nose and palate unconflicted and clear-headed as you *assemblé* the ingredients you'll need...'

'An unconflicted palate. Score one for me,' she murmured.

Their prosaic teacher was fully underway by now and his continental theatrics and charm managed to recapture the focus of the women in the room. But Zander still stared at her, eyes lightly creased.

*Stop smiling,* her eyes urged him. *We're supposed to be strangers.* Though there was something just slightly breath-stealing about the game they were playing. Pretending to be strangers. Hiding a secret from the whole room.

It was vaguely...kinky.

Which said a lot about how very not kinky her life usually was.

She forced her attention back to Chef. Did her best to listen and understand what he was saying and not pay any further attention to Zander perched at the end of the bench, deftly deflecting the interest of the two women closest to him and studying everything that was happening in the room. Parts of what the chef was saying really resonated for the scientist in her—the parts about the chemistry of food and how ingredients worked together—but they were totally overshadowed by his try-hard vocabulary and his staged theatrics, which really *didn't* work for her. She caught herself smiling more than once at something ridiculous he said or the way he gushed over his rapt female audience. She was fairly certain he wasn't actually French.

'Excuse me, Chef?' she interrupted when he paused for a rare breath and before she could change her mind. 'Will we get to cook something tonight?'

'So *enthousiaste*,' he fawned, and she groaned. '*Non*, you won't get hands-on until week six. In Chef André Carlson's class we first develop *appréciation* for the art of the food, then we progress to *construction* of the food.'

And clearly much drinking of the wine, despite his own protestations.

She nodded, politely, and started counting the endless minutes until her first class was over. How would Zander feel about her dumping the first thing he'd sent her to? She glanced up. He had a resigned nothing plastered to his face. It hit her then that she was wasting two people's time on this terrible class.

'Excuse me, Chef?' This time he looked more irritated to have been interrupted mid-fake-French-stream. 'I have a terrible migraine. I'm going to have to leave.'

Much clucking of concern and old fake-French remedies for migraines later and she had her handbag over her shoulder and her feet pointing towards the door. No one cared.

'You'll need someone to walk you to your car,' Zander volunteered and then excused himself from the woman next to him. That got their attention, but he reassured them, 'I'll be right back.'

No, he wouldn't. Not if he was as dumbstruck by that class's awfulness as she was.

They practically bolted down the hall for the street door, together.

'You were going to leave me there!' he accused as they fell out into the street.

She laughed as she skipped down the steps to the footpath. 'Sorry. Every man for himself on the culinary Titanic.'

'That was awful,' he gritted. 'Why would anyone put themselves through that?'

'They looked like they were having a good enough time.'

'I can't imagine anyone coming away from that actually *appreciating* food more.'

Her laugh redoubled. 'No.'

'I take it the migraine was fake?'

'As fake as his accent. I think we should just cut our losses.'

He halted her with a warm hand to her arm. 'No. You came here tonight wanting to discover what's so special about cuisine.'

God, was he warming back up to another invitation to see his etchings?

'Let me just make a call…'

He made it. Brief and murmured, his back half to her. Then he turned and smiled at her. 'OK, all arranged.'

'What is?'

'We have a job for the night.'

'A job?'

'In a commercial kitchen. That's where you'll see what cooking is really all about.'

'I can't cook in a commercial kitchen!' She could barely boil water in her own home.

'Trust me, Georgia.' He slid his hand around behind her back and smiled. 'We won't be cooking.'

He wasn't kidding. Within fifteen minutes they were installed up to the elbows in suds in the back of the busy kitchen of an Italian restaurant and they'd washed more dishes in less time than she'd even dirtied in her whole life. But she didn't even notice.

The owner of the restaurant where Zander had called in his favour elevated the usual dishwashers to kitchen assistants for the night and had one of his demi-chefs explain everything happening in the kitchen for their benefit.

She and Zander eavesdropped on every word between suds.

And his digital recorder—totally approved by the owner— captured it for EROS' segment.

The kitchen ran like a ballet. Every item on the menu cho-reographed; every technique a combination of hard-learned steps. Every resulting dish a work of art, never the same twice.

The chef—a real, proper chef this time, with a real accent— yelled at everyone just enough to keep them moving, and didn't hesitate to yell at his trainee dishwashers if she and Zander fell behind. She felt more welcome being yelled at in this kitchen than being fawned over in the last one. The clunk and clatter of knives and pots and whisks merged with the hiss of frying fat and draining pasta pots to create a symphony of experience that had so much more excitement and interest than just how to cook a good cordon bleu.

And such language! The night was an education for more reasons than one. She loved even that. Though she knew Zan-der's editors would be busy with the bleep button.

The symphony and ballet went on for hours. She grew trans-fixed trying to take it all in even as her feet started first to ache, then protest and finally give up and just burn. But her sore feet were the least of their worries. A whole dish went wrong and sent the kitchen into desperate chaos catching back up and she felt the adrenaline of the race, the thrill of contributing, the deep satisfaction of getting the replacement meals out in time. Even if her role was only keeping the clean cutlery coming.

And now the night was nearly over. The last customers were on their desserts and only one big pot bubbled away in the half-empty kitchen. The promoted-for-a-night assistants were more than happy to cook something simple for the people who'd triggered their unexpected elevation, and Georgia and her sore feet were more than happy to be cooked for by them.

Who knew, maybe the two men would get to do it more often now that they'd been ripped out of their sudsy pigeonhole.

She'd watched them make it from scratch. Pasta. Carefully mixed, rolled, strung, cooked. And the leftover sauce from the night's bolognese. The owner-chef passed through and plated up for both of them, a modest bowl for Georgia and an enormous mound for Zander. With a barrage of hasty Italian between.

'Are you pregnant?' she joked, settling her heat-wrinkled fingers around one of the forks she'd washed herself.

He chuckled. 'I'm carb-loading.'

'Which is what for the uninitiated?' She curled a dozen strands of beautifully shaped pasta around her fork.

'The day before a big run you load your body up on carbohydrates and water to ensure it's full of energy.'

'Energy you burn off running fifty kilometres?'

'Exactly.'

'Where will you run tomorrow?'

He hesitated answering. She didn't let her sigh show. 'You don't like to talk about it much.'

'I'm unaccustomed to anyone asking. It's usually just my thing.'

That rankled just a tiny bit. 'I'm not going to invite myself along again if that's what you're worried about.'

'I know,' he replied as she slid a fully loaded fork into her mouth.

*Oh, my God...* She liked spaghetti. She'd even been excited enough once or twice to make her own lumpy Napolitano sauce in her slow cooker. But this...*this*! The combination of home-cooked bolognese and minutes-old, fresh pasta on top of the bone weariness, hollow stomach and flat-footed agony of having stood doing dishes for hours...

'This is amazing, Zander!'

'One of my favourite bolt holes.'

She glanced up at him. His choice of words struck her. 'Where do you bolt from?'

How could a shrug be so tense? 'Life. Work. Everything.'

She could understand that, if the man bursting out of his office was a regular occurrence.

'We could both do worse than running our workplaces the way Chef ran this kitchen,' she said softly.

'What do you mean?'

'Firm. High expectations. But fair. And everyone here was working with him, not despite him.'

Zander looked around the near-empty kitchen. The two assistants had already removed any hint of evidence that their meal had ever existed. The way they were demolishing their pasta, it very soon wouldn't.

'What makes you think it's not like that already?' he asked.

'Something one of your staff said when I was in your office.' She'd been there a few times over the weeks finalising the list with Casey, so that was suitably broad. He wouldn't know who amongst his team it was. 'They said I was a lamb to the slaughter.'

He blinked at her, then recommenced eating his meal. But his brows remained low.

'Not saying I agree with them. You've been nothing but nice to me.' If one had a liberal definition of *nice*. 'But, you know, clearly they thought you were going to make things hard for me.'

He thought about that some more. 'It's what they would expect.'

'Why?'

'Because it's what they know.'

Sadness washed across his expression and then vanished. 'Why do you make things hard for them?'

'Because I'm their boss. The network delivers the good news and I deliver and implement the bad. It's what I get paid for.'

'That's a miserable kind of job. Why do you do it?'

He laughed. 'You've seen where I live.' One of London's better suburbs.

'And you've seen where I live. So what? That's not who we are.'

His eyes grew assessing. 'Really? Your apartment exterior is modest and plain, but well kept. Someone cares for that building. I'd hazard a guess that the inside would be the same. Everything in its place, nothing unessential. Isn't that exactly as you are?'

She stared at her near-empty bowl. 'Is that how I strike you? Orderly and dull?'

'You strike me as someone who's stuck in a rut. Maybe who has been for some time.'

She lifted her chin. 'Ruts come in all shapes and suburbs. Besides, you shouldn't judge a book by its cover.'

He lifted his chin to match hers. 'Really? Care to put your money where your mouth is?'

'You want to bet on it?' She frowned.

'I want to see it.'

*Oh.*

'When?'

'How about now?'

'It's not tidy—'

'Yes, it is.'

*Yes...it is.* She sighed. 'You have a race in the morning.'

His eyes grew serious. 'I'm not proposing sleeping over, Georgia, just a quick look.'

Heat flared up the back of her neck and she worked hard to keep it from flooding around to the front. She *had* made the immediate assumption that this was some kind of line. Zander Rush was a fit and sexy man. And so of course it wasn't a come-on. Not for her.

'I just meant…it's late.'

'I don't run until noon. And it's too late for you to be taking the tube.'

It wasn't, but she didn't mind the idea of a comfortable Jag ride home. She wasn't ready for their first night to be over.

*The* first night. Not *their* first night.

'OK, I'll take the lift.' And show him the inside of her flat for a minute or two. And then he and his fascination would be gone. 'Thank you.'

They rinsed their dishes in the cooling water, thanked the chef who was enjoying a drink with his team out in the now-empty restaurant, and headed out into the dark.

'You want to drive?' he asked.

No. She wanted him to drive. Inexplicably. So of course, she said, 'Yes, please.'

He pulled his coat collar up as high as possible against the cool April weather. 'One of these days you'll stop being so courteous and I'll know we're finally getting somewhere.'

The drive took about twenty minutes. Conversation was light between them but not because they had nothing to say. She just didn't feel the need to say anything. And besides, the scrumptious dinner was kicking in and metabolising down into a warm goo that leached through her veins. She worked hard to keep her focus sharp while driving Zander's land-yacht.

'Who else lives here?' he murmured quietly as they crossed into the shared entry hall of her apartment building.

She ran her fingers along the four letterboxes by the door.

'Two students, a long-term resident…' She traced the last box; its lettering was cool and smooth under her touch. 'And me.'

She led him through to the back of the entry hall where her door was.

If Mr Lawler came out for one of his late-night cigarettes now he'd be in for quite a surprise. Not that she'd never had a man here before, but not like this…tiptoeing in late at night. All clandestine and exciting…

She turned her key, wiggled it, put her shoulder to the door, and popped it quietly open. It swung inwards into the darkened apartment. 'Acquired touch,' she whispered.

Why was she so breathless? Was it just because she was walking into her home with a virtual stranger? Or was it because she loved her apartment? It was so…her. So if he judged it, he judged her.

She flicked on the light.

His eyes scanned the room, giving nothing away. 'This is…'

Crazy and shambolic? Nothing like the outside? She saw it how a stranger must, the explosions of random colour, the stacks of books and home-beautiful magazines. Trailing plants everywhere.

He touched the nearest green frond. 'How do you get them to look like this inside?'

She crossed to the double doors opening onto her small courtyard and pulled back the blind. 'I rotate them every day. One day in, three days out.'

His eyes swung to her. 'How many do you have?'

It was too dark to see outside, too dark for him to discover the full extent of her guilty pleasure. 'I'm kind of the crazy cat-lady of trailing ferns.'

He looked around him again, then found her eyes. 'It's not what I expected.'

That could mean anything, but she chose to interpret it positively. 'Surprise!'

His focus fell onto the stack of brightly packaged CDs

stacked up on her corner desk. He crossed to them. 'Are you studying?'

'Espionage through history. I'm getting ready for the spy class.'

He flipped one of the CDs over and read the description of the lectures. 'You're doing homework before the class?'

'I like to be prepared. And I'm really looking forward to the spy classes.'

One brow quirked. 'As distinct from the others?'

Heat rose and consumed her in the tiny apartment. 'I listen to them when I'm gardening. On the bus to and from work. Or when I'm walking.'

'You walk?'

'Regularly.'

'Where?'

What was this, the Inquisition? 'Anywhere I haven't been before. Deep in some wood somewhere.'

His nod was distracted. He suddenly looked intensely uncomfortable.

'I bought these with my own money.' In case that was what was putting that deep frown on his face.

'Why?'

'Because your money is for things that interest your listeners.'

He turned towards her. 'You don't have to hide things from me. If there's something you want to do, do it. The money is for you.'

It wasn't him she was hiding from. She took the CDs out of his hands. 'It's not... I feel like these are normal me, not new improved me. Besides, you've already indicated that the things I'm interested in aren't that...exciting.' She cleared her throat. 'For your listeners.'

His eyes fell on her heavily. Searching and conflicted.

'Coffee?' she asked just to break the silence.

He broke free of her gaze, bustling towards the door as

though this were all the most terrible inconvenience. 'No. I should get going.'

And suddenly she was feeling self-conscious for agreeing to *his* request. She followed him back out into the hall. 'Thanks for the lift.'

'No problem.'

He had to stop at the door to the street to negotiate the intricate series of locks. If not for that, she wondered if he might have just flown down the stairs and path and been gone. She opened it for him and stood below the arch.

'And for the restaurant. It was fantastic to see.'

'We'll find you new cooking classes. You don't have to go back to the French guy.'

'The not-French guy...'

'Right.' He practically squirmed on her doorstep. Confusion milled around them both. This *had* been his idea? Or had she just misunderstood?

'Well, see you next time, then,' she said quietly.

'OK. 'Night, Georgia.'

And then he was gone. Not quite running as she'd imagined, but certainly making good time on those long, marathon legs. Into his car and away. Expensive tail lights glowing until they turned onto the high street in the distance.

And still she stood there.

OK. That was just weird. Their whole night had been genial enough, the silence in the ride over here mutual and comfortable. Or so she'd thought. She'd only offered him coffee, not exactly controversial.

*Modest, plain but well kept.* Was that what he'd been expecting her place to be like? She resecured the front door and turned off the porch light, then crossed back to her gaping apartment door, assessing the inside critically. Shambolic but not unclean. She had nothing to be particularly embarrassed about.

Maybe he had a plant phobia.

She sighed. Maybe this was a Year of Georgia test. See how she was going with the judgement of others. Not well, apparently.

She cared what people thought. She didn't run her life by it, but criticism did impact on her. Especially someone like Zander Rush. Rich, powerful men might not particularly matter to her professional life, but this one mattered to her personal life. She had a year ahead of her with Zander, they were going to be in each other's faces a reasonable amount. She'd really rather not have that time be tense and awkward.

And below that, somewhere deeper that she only peeled a corner back on, lay her secret fear: that the same *lack* that made Daniel not interested in marrying her might have occurred to Zander as he stood here in her little apartment. Some undefined deficiency. Was she too geeky? Too dull? Was she so left-of-normal that even a man whose connection to her was only professional felt the need to run for the hills? If so, he was in for a disappointing year.

There was only so much that reinvention was going to fix.

Zander tossed his keys and wallet into the shallow dish by his bed and then took himself off for a shower. As hot as he could stand it. Desperate to scald himself clean of the sudden tingle of awareness he'd experienced standing in Georgia's apartment just half an hour before. He'd learned to live with the perpetual hum of sensual responsiveness that resonated whenever she was around, but this was different, this was...

*Interest.*

The prickle of intrigue and the glow of connection. So much more than just sexual. Unexpected, unwanted, and unacceptable. And the slither of empathy, that his words made her doubt herself, made her so defensive.

He stood under the hot, thumping water and let it stream over his head.

*The crazy cat-lady of trailing ferns.*

Of all the things to suddenly bring this *burbling* inside him to the surface...that little touch of self-deprecation, her modesty about her lived-in, loved-in apartment, her raw defence of a place that was clearly special to her. That was clearly *her*. She defended her property and herself with a gentle kind of resignation. As though she knew full well that she didn't fit the conventional moulds and was reconciled with that.

And he was there telling her that her mould wasn't interesting enough for his listeners.

Then showering himself raw just half an hour later because of how interesting it *was* to him.

Hypocrite.

His life was so laden with false, socially aggressive people, all hungry to climb ladders that they had to jostle for. So full of noise and gloss and professional veneer. He did his best to limit his exposure to it to his working hours, running from it—literally—on weekends, but when you worked as much as he did it had a way of just dominating your consciousness.

Until you stood in the middle of someone's small, packed greenhouse of an apartment and felt as if you'd just walked into some kind of emotional resort. Far from everything and everyone.

Until you breathed in for the first time in fifteen years.

Zander shut off the water, towelled off, and stepped out into his bedroom. Carefully styled by the owner before him, all beige and tones of brown and harmless neutrals he'd never bothered to change. Then he walked out of the hall, into every room one by one, growing increasingly incredulous.

Not one single plant, anywhere? Seriously?

He kept looking, kept not finding one. Until he did. A small cactus in a pot that Casey had given him before she'd twigged to the fact that gifts between them weren't going to do anything but make their relationship more awkward. He'd plonked it on his kitchen window sill and never given it another thought. It survived only on the steam issued by his coffee maker. And maybe the dishwasher.

But it survived.

The similarity to his thorny, parched heart was ironic.

He flicked a switch and lit up the entire length of his rambling back garden. Did it even count if you paid someone to tend it for you? If the most you did was cut roses to take to your aging mother and the only time you walked through it was on a shortcut back from the local coffee house?

The fun Georgia would have if let loose in there...

He killed the lights, plunging the whole garden and that train of thought back to darkness.

There would be no letting loose. There'd be no more curious visits to her apartment. He'd only gone to assure himself that her home would have been as lacking in personality on the inside as the exterior. As some kind of ward against finding her interesting.

Well, that had bitten him well and truly in the arse.

He couldn't blame his complicated mess of interest and appreciation and affection on her botched proposal any longer. Georgia Stone might have started out as the embodiment of every professional and ethical compromise he'd made on his meteoric corporate trajectory—and he still felt the cuts every time someone praised him for the sensational PR surrounding her proposal—but she was rapidly morphing into something else.

A living, breathing, *haunting* reminder of the man he used to be. Before the heartbreak of being jilted by Lara. Before the humiliation that drove him headlong into his intense professional life, and the professional life that drove him headlong into his insane training regime just to balance out all the noise. Before all of those things left no room for an actual life. He missed life. And moments like tonight didn't help him to keep that longing safely tucked away where it couldn't gnaw at him.

But work did. And running did. And he had plenty of both to be getting on with this weekend.

Neither of which were served by flashes of the sheer contentedness in Georgia's face as she stood in the midst of her meagre worldly possessions, richer than he could possibly conceive.

# CHAPTER FIVE

*May*

WEDNESDAY night salsa dancing was an education—a great way to discover she had three left feet and not just two. Georgia danced with a raft of partners of various coordination—some more patient than others—but never Zander. He was always careful to share the love around with strangers, favouring the much older or much younger and discouraging the interest of anyone in the middle.

Her, most especially.

She'd only made the mistake of asking him once.

*We're here to work*, he'd said.

Right.

This was the side of him his staff saw. Officious. Distant. Work-centric. That other side of him that she'd glimpsed only lasted as long as it took him to tire of the novelty of following her to endless courses and classes and experiences. The more they did together, the less civil he became.

So maybe she'd been demoted to minion in his mind?

The only blessing was that the segments he was producing from their time together in class didn't reflect any of his impatience and ennui. She'd moved past her instinctive cringe at hearing herself as others heard her and let herself enjoy reliving the classes through Zander's eyes. His ears. His art. Because while they were commercial by necessity, they were also pretty good. Floating out across the airwaves once a month.

And she'd busied herself finding things to do in class that didn't amplify this awkward…blech…between them.

Thursday night was Michelin-starred restaurants night and she'd become adept at pretending she didn't know the handsome man at the next table. And at eating alone. There was a certain loveliness that London's service staff reserved for a woman taking a meal by herself. At first she worried that it was pity, but then she realised they just wanted to make her solo experience as nice as possible. She got twice the smiles and extra free bread that Zander did. That pleased her to an unnaturally high degree.

Friday night wine appreciation was at least a blessing because it meant their minds and mouths were both fully occupied and so conversation between herself and Zander really wasn't an option, anyway. But at least the wine class provided quality alternatives in the shape of other men to talk to. And women—but they never got much of a rise from Zander. It was the men that really got up his nose, presumably because it was impacting on the quality of their Year of Georgia project.

She wasn't supposed to be on the hunt. She was supposed to be discovering who she was. And it was working; it turned out she was a woman who liked to goad surly, silent executive types.

She turned to Eric on her left and laughed loudly at something he said. Even he looked surprised to have been that amusing. He developed software apps for a living and he and his techie-mate Russell, on her right, had decided their circle of friends really needed to include someone other than the pair of them. And preferably with the X chromosome.

Hence the wine appreciation.

The three of them developed a healthy symbiosis—they honed their flirting skills on her and she let them. It felt good being appreciated by someone and not just tolerated by Zander. Buoyed by their company, she sniffed and she sipped and she spat and she was careful never to quaff in front of Zander. And, it turned out, she had a pretty good nose and palate for identifying wine types. Unlike cooking, which she'd still not really mastered at all. Though, she wasn't above quietly taking the mickey.

She agitated the wine in her hand until it made large circles in the balloon glass and its aroma climbed. She waved the whole lot under her nose.

'Truculent. With undertones of—' she looked around for inspiration and her eyes fell on the earrings of the woman across from her '—amber and—' she searched again and her eyes fell on Zander '—oak moss.'

Because that was what he always smelled like to her. One of her forests.

Russell's eyes narrowed. 'Really?'

Eric just laughed. 'She's lying.'

She leaned closer to both of them. 'Truly, it just smells like good red wine.' She tossed her sample back. 'Yep. Good.'

All three of them laughed and she turned to place her empty glass onto the cleaning tray, but as she did so she lifted her eyes and encountered Zander's, intense and assessing.

As usual.

Class wound up not long after and she farewelled her friends happily. They always asked her out with them after class. She always declined.

'You can go,' Zander said, suddenly close behind her as Eric and Russell left. 'You're off the clock.'

She bit down her retort. How typical that about the only thing he'd said to her all evening was boorish. 'If I wanted to go I would go. I wasn't waiting for permission.'

'It's Friday night.'

'And this class is my Friday night activity.' Poor effort though it was. She slid her coat more firmly on and headed onto the street.

He stuck to her heels. 'They're going to go off you if you don't give them something.'

She turned and glared. 'Something? A bit of leg? A flash of cleavage?'

'Not what I meant.' He glowered.

'I know what you meant. I'm not interested in anything beyond their company in class.' And—just quietly—the impact it had on Zander. Getting his blood up was at least better than stony silence. 'This isn't about dating, remember.'

'I was wondering if you did.'

She spun and huffed in equal measures. 'I have to talk to someone. You're the only person I know and we're strangers here.' And increasingly everywhere. 'Some of them are going to be men. It's not dating strategy.'

He just grunted. 'This is my Friday night, too, you know.'

She stared. 'I do know.'

'So it would just be useful to keep everything professional. On mission.'

*On mission?* 'I'm not allowed to have a good time, at all? Doesn't that defeat the purpose?'

'The purpose is you getting back on track. Learning new things. Reinventing.'

A month of standoffishness took its toll. 'I'm not sure that you appreciate how hard some of this is for me. Walking alone into a room full of people I don't know. Striking up friendships. I would so much rather be at home curled up with a good book.'

His eyes clouded over. Was he thinking? Or just bored? 'How hard?'

'It's…difficult. I'm not social, like you. I like to meet people, find out about them, but I'm just not really good at it. It's work.' And developing those skills was part of her twelve-month plan but it was a case of chicken and egg. She needed the skills to be able to walk into any social situation, but she wasn't going to develop the skills unless she kept walking into those situations.

He looked truly astonished. 'I didn't realise. You make it look so easy.'

Was he kidding? 'It's exhausting.'

'Would it be easier to have a friend along?'

'Yes.'

'Let's do that, then. This isn't supposed to be punishment. We can tweak the budget.'

It felt like it some nights. She let out a long breath and added yet another humiliation to her very many. 'I don't have anyone to bring. Not every week.' She could probably get any one of her friends away from their parenting responsibilities once, maybe twice. But weekly? Sometimes twice weekly? Not a prayer. This was the sort of thing she used to rely on Dan for.

Her social handbag.

The great mess that was them struck her again. *Imagine if he'd said yes...*

'I'm here anyway,' he said. 'I'll do it.'

Her heart flipped like a fish. 'You wanted to remain impartial.'

'The situation has changed.'

'You know you'll have to speak to me. Not just interview me or record me talking to others.'

Impatience leaked out of him. 'I've been trying to keep things professional.'

'What's unprofessional about having the occasional conversation?'

'If you're talking to me then you're not talking to everyone else.'

It was a valid point. She was just as likely to talk to him all night given half a chance. But it didn't make it feel any better. 'I promise to multitask. If you promise not to scowl at me the whole time.'

'I don't scowl.'

'You're doing it now. That's just going to scare away anyone that comes close enough to talk to.'

'They'll just assume I'm one of many dates who are there under sufferance.'

'A date with a digital recorder?' He'd started bringing them along to the second and third sessions of each activity. The first was pure reconnaissance.

'That reminds me. I'm going to start recording next week. We have permission.'

'Make sure you get Eric and Russell. Maybe a bit of fame will increase their chances with the ladies.'

He grunted. 'I don't think anything will increase their chances.'

'They're nice men.'

'They try too hard.'

'Doing this *is* hard. For a lot of people coming to one of these things is either last resort or a kind of admission of fail- ure. That you can't be cultured and interesting without help.'

His eyes narrowed. 'Is that how you feel?'

She studied him, wondering if she could trust him. She would have told Zander off a month ago, no problem. But cor- porate Zander wasn't anywhere near as approachable. Then again, the Year of Georgia was all about taking risks.

'I'm smart, I have a good job, excellent work ethic, property. I'm passable-looking. So what's wrong with me?'

Zander opened his mouth but she barrelled onwards. 'Maybe he would have liked me more if I was sportier, wittier, pret- tier. Maybe there's a whole range of things that other women out there can do that I can't.'

'This is about Daniel?'

'No. Daniel is Everyman, he's just a symbol. But he was a man so like me I thought we were a perfect fit, so to not even be good enough for him...'

'I thought you were doing this for you. The Year of Georgia.'

She glared at him. 'First—as you've so carefully pointed out—I'm doing this for you. Because your contract says I have to. But right behind that *is* me. And part of me is wondering why I'm not more popular with men. Or with other women. Why I don't have more friends. Or a family yet. Or a better job. Or why my life isn't like other people's.'

He shook his head. 'What do you imagine happens in other people's lives that's so special and different?'

'I don't know. Cool stuff. Busy, interesting, challenging stuff?'

'That's just dressing. Most people's lives are exactly the same underneath. The same worries about finances, their careers, the same family dramas. Only the outer coating changes.'

'What about you—rich, popular, respected, in demand, powerful? You can do whatever you want and go wherever you want whenever you want. That's not the same as everyone else.'

He stopped again and faced her. 'I haven't had a holiday in five years because the network believes the station will collapse if I walk away from it for a moment. I have a big, expensive house that someone else decorated and I can go weeks without even going into rooms that aren't my bedroom, bathroom, and study. I have parents who live in a perpetual state of warfare. That power you covet means people either shy away from me or suck up to me. So my life is riddled with its own hassles but I don't dwell on it and I certainly don't voice it. I just get on with it.'

Such a confession, after weeks of standoffish Zander, struck her deep. Was that really how he felt about his life? Maybe the trappings of success and popularity really were just that.

'Are you saying I should just suck it up?' And shut up.

Maybe that was exactly what she needed to hear? Perhaps her self-reflection was just self-indulgence in disguise.

'I'm saying all the classes in the world aren't going to make your life better, because life isn't something you apply like make-up. It's something you grow and tend. Like a garden.'

Her present life would make a pretty straggly, restricted garden. But a life filled with makeovers and clubbing and movie premieres wasn't all that brilliant, either, unless you happened to discover a new passion. They were just flashy statues amongst the weeds.

She blinked. Thought. Smiled. 'That's kind of profound. We should have recorded that.'

'I have my moments.'

'So am I wasting my time?' Because she certainly hadn't discovered a hidden passion for anything they'd done so far.

'Not if they're things you've always wanted to do.'

They weren't, really. They were things she thought she *should* do. Things EROS' listeners might like. Things that she felt Zander might have expected her to do.

'How locked in is the schedule?'

He squinted one eye. 'Some of them are all booked and paid, some transferable. Why?'

'I think I need to tweak them. To be more…me.'

He smiled. 'OK. Just talk to Casey.'

Just like that? How strange that she felt so uncomfortable asking for what she wanted. When it was so straightforward.

They walked on.

'So, how come you don't fix your life, then?' Her words came out as mist on the cool air. 'Make changes? If you believe so much in the garden of life.'

He shrugged. 'Not everyone wants a garden. Or the hassle of tending it. Sometimes a single focus is just easier.'

His work. Of course. 'But you love running. Your weekends are always full. That's at least a small garden *bed*, surely.'

'I don't do it because I'm passionate about it.'

'Why then?'

'For the silence.'

Hours and hours of silence as his machine of a body put foot in front of foot. 'Just you and the voices in your head, huh?'

He smiled. 'Right. That's all the company I need.'

Suddenly she felt very self-conscious to be standing here taking up his silence. Although she suspected he'd only be working anyway. Fortunately, a tube entrance loomed.

'Well, I guess I should—'

'I have a garden,' he blurted. 'An actual one, I mean.'

She figured that the big house in Hampstead Heath came with a big plot of land. 'OK.'

'I'd like you to see it.'

'Why?'

He paused before answering. 'Because it's lovely. It should be appreciated.'

The man who didn't even use the rooms in his house? She couldn't picture him getting out in the garden. But maybe this whole contract arrangement had some kind of implied reciprocity that she hadn't considered.

Or maybe this was some kind of peace overture. If it was, she'd take it.

'Sure. I'd like to see it.'

'Maybe you can give me some tips on what to do with it.'

'I'm not a landscaper—'

'I'm not looking for shape, I'm looking for soul.' Surprise flooded his face, as if he'd never considered that before.

'A soulful garden. Well, I'm sure I can at least give you some tips.'

'Don't underrate yourself. Look at what you do in your back yard. The life you've invested that three square metres with.'

She considered that. 'When do you want me to come by?'

'How about next Saturday?'

'Aren't you running?'

'I'm doing a night run. I have all day free.'

All day? 'Just how big is this garden?'

He smiled and ushered her onto the tube steps. 'You'll see.'

*Enormous* was the answer. Gi-flipping-gantic. At least four times the size of the house sitting like a stone sentry on its western edge and that was already very big.

Georgia turned a slow three-sixty from her spot in the middle of the garden's first chamber and surveyed the extraordinary, neglected space. Not physically neglected—the turf was mowed and the pruning regular. But Zander was right: this garden lacked any kind of soul.

'This is amazing.' She looked at him. 'Do you truly not use it?'

'I shortcut through it from the main street.'

Sacrilege. To have a garden like this, to have it be all your own and then never use it.

'There's a lot you could do here.'

'I have brown thumbs.'

'You have something better. Deep pockets. You could hire a team.'

'I don't want a team. I want you.'

She glanced at him.

'Someone like you,' he rushed on. 'Someone with passion for it. To look after it.'

The awkwardness of the moment flailed around between them. *I want you.* She'd practically given herself whiplash snapping her head around to look at him.

'I don't think you'll have any trouble finding someone to do more than just mow and prune. I could give you some names if you like.'

Hers would have been at the top of the list for anyone but him. What she wouldn't give to get to tinker in this garden.

'That would be great.'

She basked in the heat coming off him in the cool mid-morning air. Maybe carb-loading turned you into a furnace. Whatever the cause, she caught herself swaying towards his warmth.

She turned the unintentional move into a full body spin before he noticed it and looked again at the magnificent potential all around her.

'I have hedgehogs,' he murmured.

Her eyes fluttered shut. Of course he did. That was just the final nail in the coffin. 'This is wasted on you,' she said, bleak.

But her soft groan must have communicated her affinity for the space because he didn't take offence.

'Because I don't use it?'

'Because you don't love it. This garden—' she turned back to the west '—this stunning house… These should be in the hands of someone who worked hard their whole life to have it. Not someone who only uses the garden for short cuts and who uses just two of the rooms.' Yet paid a premium for them. 'Why do you stay?'

She'd asked him before but he hadn't answered.

'Come on in,' he hedged. 'I'll show you inside.'

Maybe she'd been rude to say it like that—out loud, to his face—but she truly didn't understand how someone could have all this and not want to spend every waking moment in it.

Inside was the carefully styled twin of outside. Perfectly maintained, but utterly soulless. Like a short-term executive rental.

'Where's your study?' She could hardly ask to see his bedroom, but she was desperate to get a sense of him. Of who Zander Rush really was.

He led her up a sweeping, curved staircase to the upper floor and along a spotless landing. It struck her then that he'd be better off closing off the unused rooms and throwing cloths over all the furniture. She suggested it.

'No. I don't want to live like that. It doesn't take my cleaner long to dust and vacuum. This way it's ready if people come over unexpectedly.'

She slid her eyes sideways. 'Does that happen often?'

Something told her it didn't. She had the strangest feeling she was one of only a few people this house ever saw.

Again, criminal.

A house like this should be seen. By someone.

He paused outside a door and looked at her. 'Welcome to the inner sanctum.'

It felt like that. Privileged. Rare. Something about the air that whooshed out as he swung opened the big timber door. She thought to see some kind of expansive library with ladders and a massive antique desk and dead animal heads lining the wall. Something as grand as the house. She couldn't have been more wrong. It was small but not tiny. Opulently carpeted, tasteful timber desk at the far end, and an array of antique bookcases of all different sizes and shapes and filled with books.

It was charming. And warm. And personal.

And such an unexpected thing given the rest of the house.

She stepped forward and trailed her fingers along the various surfaces. He watched her silently.

'It's lovely,' she said, conscious that he seemed to expect some kind of verdict. 'And comfortable; I can see why you spend a lot of time in here.'

Not as much as the garden, if this were her house and not his. She'd build a nest in the conservatory and hibernate in there.

'I get much more done here at home than at the station.'

'I'm surprised you don't work from home more.'

'There's only so much alone time a man can take.' He smiled. 'Even me.'

She couldn't imagine a busier or noisier Monday to Friday than working in a crowded radio station. She crossed around behind his desk and studied the carved bust by the window. 'A relative? Some famous broadcasting type?'

He shook his head. 'It was in the house when I bought it. I had it moved in here because it seemed a fitting sort of decoration for a study.'

How sad. A beautiful house full of someone else's memories. She turned and skimmed her eyes over the paperwork scattered around a closed laptop on his desk. None of it interested her, but a colourful mini-poster pressed to the surface of the desk by a chunk of granite did.

His next event notice. Hadrian's Wall, Gilsland to Bowness.

The following weekend. She'd never seen a marathon in progress. And it was a public event…

She conveniently ignored the fact that she'd promised him she wouldn't ask to go to one of his events. And that not telling him was just plain creepy.

'Do you cook in your kitchen?' she blurted, steering her focus—and his—away from the notice on his desk.

'With fifteen restaurants in walking distance there's little need, but yes, I have used the oven.'

'I was thinking more about the kettle. I'd love a coffee while I make that list of landscapers.'

And get a better feel for the man himself, and what might have happened to him in his life to make him such an under-committed, over-achieving workaholic.


'Best. Course. Ever!' Georgia said as she hunkered down on the opposite side of a half-destroyed door, chest heaving and brandishing her heavy artillery up near her face.

Zander chuckled from the darkness beyond the flimsy doorway. 'I don't believe it. Have we finally found something you'd have done if you had free choice?'

'Totally! Who knew I'd be so fast at assembling a gun?' She tightened the harness crossing her chest until it was snug again.

'Or cracking a code.'

She leaned back into the artfully decorated set designed to look like a shelled-out building. Less shabby-chic and more… Afghanistan-ic. 'Makes up for being such a lousy femme fatale, I guess.'

'Not everyone's cut out for seduction,' he threw away in the brief moment he peered his head around the doorway to assess the enemy location.

Some of the joy sucked out of her day. Believing it herself was different from having it pointed out by a man. By this man.

'Ready?' he checked.

She shook her doubts free and readied her weapon. 'Locked and loaded.'

'On my count…'

God, this was fun. She braced herself against the wall and waited for 'three'. When it came she surged to her feet and sprinted across the open courtyard, as damaged and rubble-strewn as the rest of the set, with Zander hard up behind her. Halfway across, one of the yellow team popped up out of no-where and aimed right at them both. Georgia dived to her left, crashing into a fake rubbish skip and sliding around behind it only to come face to face with one of her instructors, kitted out in the garb of the yellow team.

'Bang,' he said, popping the barrel of his fake gun hard up to her laser-tag and firing. The lights came on in the arena. He gave her his hand. 'The good news is, you were the last of your team to die. If that's any consolation.'

Yay for her! Last woman standing.

'What happened to Zander?' she puffed.

'The big guy? He got hit by the shot you dodged.'

Her breath caught. *Whoops.*

Sure enough, the look Zander threw her as she stepped out from behind the skip was incredulous. 'I can't believe you let me take that hit!' he accused.

She lifted her weapon and unclipped her body harness. 'I would have died.'

'But I'm your superior.'

She tipped her head back and threw him her sweetest smile. 'Superior at dying, maybe…'

He snagged her arms and pinned them behind her, stepping in hard against her body and glaring down on her. 'Isn't that just like a woman?'

The hardness of his body—all strapped up in military chest plate and pressed up so firmly against hers—stole what little breath she'd managed to recover. 'The sarcasm or the faith-lessness?' she whispered.

He tightened her hands and his eyes bored down into her soul. 'Both.'

'Just because I wouldn't die for you? Is that what you expect of people?'

A shadow crossed his features and he let her hands go. 'Is a little loyalty too much to ask?'

He was taking this very seriously for a game. 'We're highly trained agents. Loyal to no one but Queen and country.'

He grunted.

'Besides,' she breathed, 'just think how guilty you'd have felt for the rest of your military career, letting a woman die for you. It would eat you up and you'd find yourself a hermit, living in a mountain, loving no one and letting nobody in. All bitter and twisted. Useless to MI6. I saved you from a fate worse than death, Agent Rush.'

Although it occurred to her that the description wasn't all that *unlike* the real him. Minus the mountain.

His eyes narrowed. 'Also just like a woman, spinning it so I should somehow be grateful.'

'All right, people,' the instructor shouted over the din, and she stepped away from Zander's warmth, reluctantly. 'Great to see that a full day of spy training has taught you all absolutely nothing about field survival...'

Georgia laughed along with everyone else and glanced at Zander. How long had it been since she'd felt this...light? He took her weapon for her and just held it. As though it were her hand.

Of course it wasn't.

'Next week we'll be looking at surveillance gear,' the instructor continued, 'and having a go at planting a bug on someone.'

She rounded on Zander, eyes wide, and mouthed, *Yay!*

He shook his scraggy head, laughing, and stood back to let her pass in front of him back to the classroom. They stripped off their borrowed military accoutrements—very reluctantly

on Georgia's part because she'd been having herself a nice little fantasy about Zander doing that for her—and collected up
their belongings.

'Would you truly have wanted me to take that hit for you?'
she queried as they walked back towards his Jag a little later.

'It's nice to think someone would.'

She lifted her eyes to his.

'Isn't that what anyone wants?' he said. 'Someone to sac-
rifice all for them.'

'You don't seem the type,' she murmured, sliding into the
passenger seat next to him.

'I'm as susceptible as anyone to grand gestures.'

She laughed as they pulled away from the kerb. 'And you
wonder why your staff are frightened of you.' And then, at
his frown, 'If death is the only way they can get in your good
books. Even metaphorically.'

He stared ahead at the road, letting that sink in.

'You value loyalty that highly?' she risked.

He took a moment answering, but when he did it wasn't
with the same light tone that they'd been firing back and forth
since the war-games ended. 'I've not had a lot of it in my life.'

'Who from?'

But of course he wasn't going to answer that. And no matter how many hours of fun they'd just had, it didn't give her
much of a right to ask.

Instead he turned to her, brightly, and said, 'Want to grab
something to eat on the way?'

No. But she wasn't ready to go home alone, either. Maybe
she could wheedle some clues out of his assistant, Casey. Now
that she was a super spy and all. Then again, Casey probably
hadn't stayed as an assistant to a man as exacting as Zander
Rush for as long as she had by chatting casually about his private business.

She'd have to be smarter than that.

She matched the brightness of his smile. And the fakeness.

'Sure.'

# CHAPTER SIX

*June*

'It's a good ten kilometres longer than a regular marathon,' the spectator perched next to Georgia on a fold-out chair said, his eyes firmly on the bend in the road they were sitting by. 'But it's only a club-training day so it doesn't count as an ultra-marathon. It's just a good run.'

Georgia chuckled. Calling a fifty-three-kilometre run 'good' was like calling her drive up from London in her gran's borrowed car 'brief'. Though getting herself to the starting point up towards the Scottish border reminded her just how long it had been since she'd taken herself right out of London.

Too long.

So even if this was the craziest and most spontaneous of bad ideas, it at least had the rather pleasant silver lining of getting her out into fresh, brisk, northern air.

The event didn't run adjacent or even near to the actual Hadrian's Wall remains; disappointing but understandable. The past two thousand years hadn't been kind to them already, the last thing they needed was forty sweaty runners and their support crews plodding along their length. But the route trundled along paved roads and tracks and along a river in one place, and so Georgia was able to drive ahead, park, and set herself up at strategic locations with the other specta-tors to watch them go by.

She quickly realised that Zander would be in the front half of the pack, though not right at the front. Those spaces were occupied by the elite professional runners and their support crews. But he wasn't too far behind, sans support crew. Last stop she'd practically hidden in the shrubbery as the pack ran by, keen for Zander not to spot her on the side of the road. But as she'd watched him steadily plod past she realised he wasn't paying the slightest bit of attention to the spectators. He was just lost in a zone of his own. The zone that got this tough job done.

She'd had a good poke around a Roman ruin and Hadri-an's Wall itself and still been ready at this next vantage point twelve kilometres along for the moment he came jogging along the track.

'Here they come,' the man said in his thick accent, standing. He readied himself with squeeze-bottles of energy drink and a pair of bananas and stepped up to the road edge in case his run-ner needed supplies. Georgia stepped back into his considerable shadow so that she was partially screened from the runners.

Just in case.

Zander stood out in the field, both for his height and also his electric-green vest top. So she watched for that. Only about a dozen runners passed her before she saw the flash of lime and she tucked back even further into her companion's wake. As before, Zander was totally focused on the path ahead and, not expecting anyone to be out here for him, he wasn't looking for anyone. That meant his eyes were locked forward, deter-mination all over his face, and he sucked air in and blew it out steadily between the thud of his sturdy runners on the track.

A slick gloss of sweat covered most of the exposed areas of his body but instead of making him look hot and miserable, it just made him look…hot. Some men really did sweaty well and apparently buttoned-up Zander was one of them. The all-over sheen defined the contours of muscles that flexed taut with effort and made her imagine other ways he might get that sweaty. And that taut.

She shut down that thought hard as he ran past.

'Is that your guy?' the man next to her asked, his eyes still on the bend in the road up ahead, his bananas and energy drink still outstretched.

'No, he's just a friend,' she laughed. Way too brightly.

The man glanced at her quizzically, as if she'd answered a totally different question from the one he asked. 'I meant is he the one you're here cheering on?'

Heat surged into her face. 'Oh, yes.'

He turned his eyes back to the bend and waited for sight of *his* guy. Or girl. That was how little attention she'd paid to anyone but Zander. 'Next stop you're welcome to one of my squeeze-bottles if you want.'

'Thank you, no,' she said, dragging her eyes back off Zander's disappearing form. 'I'm just watching.'

She picked up her fold-a-chair.

'Well, I'll see you at the King's Arms,' the affable fellow said. 'We'll all have earned a brew by then.'

She hadn't planned on waiting at the end, she'd only thought to watch him for a bit, get a feel for this sport that he loved, and then drive the many hours back to London. But while the idea of sitting waiting to surprise him in a pub didn't appeal, the thought that what she was actually doing was tantamount to stalking appealed even less.

'Yes,' she suddenly decided. 'I'll see you there.'

Late night be damned.

She clambered her way back across the farmer's field to where her car was pulled off the road heading west—the same direction as the pack of runners.

As the afternoon wore on, Zander's form remained steady but the exertion showed in the lines around his mouth and the cords that became more pronounced in his neck and calves.

So even with all his heavy training this wasn't an easy run. The front of the pack certainly made it seem so and she was always gone by the time the rest of the pack went through. But Zander went from the front-runner in the second cluster of runners to the rear-runner in the front group with a brief, lonely stint by himself as he transitioned the ever-stretching gap between them.

Most of the other spectators went to the final checkpoint to cheer their runners across the line but Georgia headed straight for the small pub on the main street. There was no guarantee that Zander would even go there; if he valued his solitude enough he might just clamber back into his Jag and head straight back to London all puffing and sweaty.

And she'd be sitting here for nothing.

But she stayed. She wanted him to know she'd come—even if he might not be all that happy about it. She wanted him to know how much she admired his dogged determination. She wanted to know what time he'd run. Those long waits on the side of the road were great for getting a feel from the regulars on what was a good time, what the stages in the pack meant and why long-run competitors did what they did.

Curiosity and a real sense of anticipation hung with her.

She wanted him to have done well. For his sake.

The front-runners started to appear amid the small crowd in the pub. She recognised some of them since they were the ones she'd been looking at all afternoon. Their arrival at the Arms was a mini-version of the race order. Clearly there was a procedure followed by most competitors—finish, shower, pub.

Her eyes drifted to the door yet again.

The crowd grew too thick in the small pub for her to see the moment Zander actually came through the door, but they spotted each other at virtually the same moment as he turned from the bar. She sucked in a small breath, held it, and smiled.

As casual as you like. As though this were her local and he'd just happened into it. As though she weren't three hundred miles from her local. Sitting on the border of a whole other country.

'Georgia?' His confusion reached her before he did.

She stood. 'Congratulations. That was quite a run.'

'What are you doing here?' It wasn't unfriendly, but it wasn't joyous, either. Had she expected pleased?

She took a deep breath. 'I thought I'd watch you compete. I just wanted to say hello before I headed off.' *Let you know I'm not a stalker.* She reached for her handbag, realising what a desperately bad idea this all was. Not only was she not invited, but she'd intruded on his privacy. Presumed her way into his own space and sporting circle. The least she could do was keep it short.

She threaded the straps of her handbag in her fingers. 'How did you do?'

He shook his head, still trying to come to terms with her presence. 'Good. Personal best for the distance.'

She nodded. 'I saw you make that big break between the chase group and the lead,' she babbled. 'That was exciting.'

He frowned.

'I had lots of time to talk to the spectators,' she confessed, flushing. 'Ask me anything about marathon running now...'

She laughed. He didn't.

*Oh, God...* 'OK. Well, congratulations. I'm going to go.'

She didn't wait for a farewell, but started weaving her way immediately through the assembled throng. She got to the door before a hand on her shoulder stopped her.

'Georgia...'

She turned. Forced a bright smile to her face. She was getting quite good at swallowing humiliation now.

'I'm sorry,' he said. 'You being here really threw me. I'm not...' He frowned again and looked around at everyone else's support teams laughing and sharing stories. 'I'm not used to having someone here for me. Stay for a while longer?'

One foot was, literally, out of the door. It would be so easy to make an excuse about the sinking sun, the long drive home, and flee. But there was Zander, all freshly showered and apologetic and great-smelling, standing in a room full of excited buzz, inviting her to stay in it. To enjoy everyone else's post-run high. To vacation in his world for just a short while.

She scanned his face for signs of being humoured. 'Maybe for a bit, then. If you're sure you don't mind.'

'Stay. We can chalk this up to a Year of Georgia project.'

The radio promotion. Of course. Everything came back to that.

They returned to the place she'd been seated but someone had taken quick advantage of the vacant seat and slid into it. Zander turned and shepherded her through to an area behind the bar. Still busy but quieter. A small table-for-one in the far corner was empty. It didn't take him long to find a spare chair.

'I'm sorry I didn't see you out on the road,' he started, sinking onto one of the seats.

She waved away the apology. His job was to stay focused on the run, not glance at spectators in case one of them was for him. 'How do you feel after the run?'

'Always the same. Exhilarated. Drained, yet like I could do it all again. I'll feel like a conqueror for a few hours yet.'

'How many recovery days do you have?'

His lips parted in a smile and in this private little corner of the bar it was all for her. 'You really are a quick study.'

Heat filled her cheeks. 'They were quite long roadside vigils.' And lots of listening so that she didn't have to talk too much to strangers.

A genuine smile lit up his face. 'Sorry. I should have run faster.'

They chatted more about the race, the pastime, the rules, and the challenges, and Georgia found herself sinking into his obvious engagement.

'You look totally different,' she blurted.

'In civvies?'

'No. When you talk about running your entire face changes. You become so animated.'

'How do I normally look?'

She gestured to his frown. 'More like that. When you're talking about work. This Zander is…very human.'

His eyebrows shot up. 'Wow. I'm not even human in London?'

What the hell? She'd intruded on his space, she might as well go the whole way. He was a puzzle she wanted to solve. 'You're so guarded in London.'

He shrugged—totally guarded—and she regretted raising it. 'I'm in work mode when I see you. It's not London's fault.'

'Are you saying you're not yourself when you're in work mode?'

'A different part of myself.'

'So which is more you—this Zander or London Zander?'

He squinted as he thought about it. 'I work eighty hours a week so, statistically, being like this is less common. But scarcity just makes me enjoy it more.'

So he liked this side of him as much as she did.

Around them a few people stood, as if on cue. He noticed, too.

'Come on,' he said. 'We have a tradition when we run the wall.'

She followed him out of the King's Arms, feeling very comfortable and welcome in this crowd—with Zander—even though she knew how out of place she was. Such a fraud. A line of them trooped, beers in hand, down to the banks of the tidal flat that had been halfway out when she'd arrived earlier. Now water lapped right up to the banks. The groups split down into small pairs and threes and spread out along the length of the foreshore. It practically glowed with rich, dusk light.

'Solway Firth,' Zander said, taking his cue from a pair of nearby cows and sinking onto the grass. 'Best sunsets in England.'

'And Scotland,' she said, dropping down next to him and looking across the narrow expanse of water that separated the two countries. She wondered what Scots might be sitting on the opposite banks looking at England and sharing the sunset. Then she looked inland. 'What town is that down there?'

Lights twinkled where the tidal flats became a river as the sun lowered.

'Gretna Green.'

'Convenient if we were eloping.' She laughed.

But the mention of marriage dented the relaxed companionship that had blossomed between them since they sat back down at the pub.

'Have you never wanted to get married?' she asked, without thinking about how he might construe such a question. In such a context. With Gretna Green an hour's stroll away.

His answer was more of a stammer.

'Not that I'm volunteering,' she hurried. 'One misguided proposal a year is my limit. I'm just curious. You'd be quite the catch, I'd have thought.'

*Understatement.*

He took his time answering that. Or deciding how to. 'What self-respecting woman would want me and my insane schedule?'

OK, they were going with flippant, then. 'I think you'd find your postal code and credit limit would be sufficient compensation for many people.' Not to mention the body.

'Many? But not you?'

She blew a breath slowly out and stared into the orange glow of the sunset. 'I would actually be quite choosy about who I married,' she started.

'Despite all evidence to the contrary,' he murmured.

She looked at him. 'It's not like I picked Dan out of a Proposals-R-Us catalogue. I'd known him a while. I really like him as a person. He's bright and dedicated and he has really good family values.'

Would he notice the complete absence of the L-word?

'You two wanted kids?'

She snorted. 'We never discussed a week into the future, let alone years.' Which only made her proposal even more misguided. 'But he'd been looking after his sick sister and her kids for a while. So I got to see it in action. The potential.'

'Family's important to you?'

She frowned, thought about it. 'The values are important. The capacity to love and nurture something to adulthood.'

'Like plants?'

She chuckled. 'Exactly. Kids can't possibly be any fussier than ferns.'

'And that's more important to you than money or an address? Values?'

She looked at him. 'You've seen how I live. Do I strike you as someone who cares much about money or the trappings of wealth?' Or threw them around needlessly?

'Not having it is not necessarily synonymous with not wanting it,' he said. 'I used to have none and I definitely wanted it.'

'Some things are more important than money.'

'So what was the leap year promotion all about?' he asked suddenly. 'If not for the fifty grand. Why put yourself and Bradford through that?'

The sun touched the horizon. 'Did you know that sunsets are only a mirage? By the time we're seeing it touch water, the sun has already dropped below the horizon. Something to do with the curvature of the earth.'

He turned to look. And it wasn't until then that she realised how closely he'd been watching her before. But then he brought his eyes back around. 'I didn't know that. But I do recognise a subject change when I hear one.'

'It's not… I'm not comfortable talking about it.'

'Why? You think I'm going to judge you?'

'I think it might end up in the radio show.'

His face changed, then, in an instant. Back to London Zander. 'Right.'

'Zander…' Her eyes fell shut to block out his offence, but she forced them open again. 'I could barely admit to Dan why I'd done it. I can't tell the whole country.'

*I can't tell you.* Not without having to ask herself why Zander's good impression mattered more to her than Dan's.

He stared. 'Off the record.'

She dropped her eyes and plucked at the long blades of the estuary bank. 'Do you know what I do for a job?'

'You study seeds.'

'I X-ray seeds. Day in, day out, to find the ones that are incompetent. The ones that aren't viable. The ones that aren't normal. It makes a person quite proficient at spotting the signs of irregularities in others. Or in yourself.'

He stayed silent. Waited for her to connect the dots.

'Everyone I know has paired off. Started families. I felt like I was falling behind.'

There was no judgement, just curiosity. 'Is it a race?'

'No.' She had years of optimum childrearing ahead of her.
'But?'

She lifted her eyes. But the clock was ticking. 'It's hard, being with them and not being able to contribute, to understand. They all have that shared experience in common. They've become so much closer.'

'You were going to get married and have kids just to ensure you could contribute to conversation? That seems extreme.'

Put like that it sounded as ridiculous as it probably was. 'I want what they have.'

'School debt and early grey hair?'

She went to stand. 'I shouldn't expect you to understand. You have so much—'

His fingers caught her wildly flapping ones. Tugged her back down. 'George, sorry. Go on. What do they have that you want so much?'

She stared at where his long fingers held hers. Not releasing them. 'Everything. The package. A man and children to love them. A nice house in the country. Security and someone to celebrate joys with. To be wanted enough for someone to give up their freedom for.' All the things she didn't have growing up. 'Someone to fill all the holes inside me.'

'So Daniel was your gap-filler?'

She stared. Swallowed. Dropped her head with shame. 'Poor Dan. That's awful.'

'Give yourself a break. Everyone fills their gaps with something.'

'What fills yours?'

His answer was immediate. 'Work. Running.'

The only two things he did. They couldn't both be gap fillers, surely? 'What are you filling?'

He stared. 'A whole lot of empty.'

Wow. That was quite a mouthful. There was nothing to say to that. They just stared at each other as the sun fully set. Its sinking took with it some of the magic of the cusp of night and day, breaking the spell she'd been under.

How else could she excuse her revelations of the last few minutes?

She let her eyes refocus over his shoulder.

'It's gone,' she whispered.

'It'll be back tomorrow.'

She nodded. But still they didn't move.

'Why are we here, Zander?' she breathed into the fading light.

He stared at her in the rapidly cooling, darkening evening. 'Because you followed me up here?'

Half of her was terrified he'd just shrug and blame tradition. That this *thing* between them wasn't mutual. But she wasn't about to be put off so easily. 'Here, by the twinkling water as the sun sets.'

'Do you want to leave?' he murmured, eyes locked on hers.

She should. 'No.'

'Do you want to feel?'

Her lungs locked up. Suddenly the grass and cows and water around them seemed to grow as if the two of them had just hauled themselves over the top of a beanstalk, forcing them closer together and making the scant distance separating them into something negligible.

Her pulse began to hammer in earnest.

Zander raised his hand and slipped it behind her head, lowering his forehead to rest on hers. His heat radiated outwards. His eyes drifted shut.

She hesitated for only a moment, then turned her face to rub her jaw along his, twisting inwards, seeking out the lips that hunted for hers. The full lips she'd been wanting to taste since she'd seen them stained with bolognese sauce and a smile in the restaurant kitchen.

Was that how long she'd been wanting it for?

Her breath came heavy and fast and mingled with his. Then she turned inwards, drawn by the plaintive breath that was her name on his lips. Their mouths touched. Sensation sparked between them and birthed a flame, hot and raw. Zander pressed their lips more firmly together, leaned into her. Curled his fingers into the hair at her nape. Georgia pressed a hand to the damp, cool earth and used it to lever herself closer to him, to hold the connection fast. To explore and taste and experience. His breath became hers. Her breath sustained them both. She kissed him harder. Greedy for his taste.

Desire raged up around them as though the setting sun had boiled the waters of the firth and they'd spilled over to the banks where they lay.

And, yes, it was *lay*. Somehow, between one desperate breath and the next, they'd sunk down to the grass and Zander twisted half over her. She couldn't remember getting there. Her entire consciousness was consumed with the press of his mouth against hers and the weight of his body on hers. He leaned on his elbows, both hands free to tangle in her hair, his mouth free to roam wherever it pleased.

And, boy, did it please.

Her head spun, her chest squeezed, her insides squirmed. Every cell in her body cried out to just merge with his. As though they recognised their chemical equal.

It wasn't until his thigh slid down between hers that reality intruded.

For both of them.

She twisted her face away from his and sucked in a breath of fresh coastal air. Sweeter and colder than anything they got in London. It helped to clear her muddled head, just a little.

Zander lifted his lips and stared down at her. Speechless.

'Um...' What more could she say?

*Where the hell had that come from?*

One minute they were talking and the next she was crawling down his throat, hungry for more of the best kiss she'd ever had.

He pressed back up, grinding closer where it really counted and sending a new wave of heat to her cheeks. He twisted sideways and his heavy, sexy weight lifted off her.

She missed him instantly.

She sat up and blew air slowly through swollen lips.

'Georgia, I—' He cut himself off to clear his throat.

She couldn't bear to hear him apologise, or declare it a mistake or express remorse. Not for a kiss like that. Not him. So she jumped in before he could start again, laughing lightly. Faking heavily. 'Chalk it up to your post-race high? All those conquering impulses?'

He'd conquered her all right—like a Viking. And that thought triggered a rush of new images and sensations. God, how she'd love to just lie back and concede defeat.

Weighing up his choices showed in his face, even in the dim light. 'We could say that.'

She took a breath.

'Or we could acknowledge the chemistry that's been between us since we met.'

*Acknowledge it* sounded a lot like forgiving it. Releasing it. Ignoring it.

'Since we met?' Though she still remembered the spark as he'd handed her the coat out at Wakehurst.

'It had to come to a head at some time.'

'You ignored me for so many weeks.'

'I was trying to ignore *it*. Not you. Our relationship was a professional one.'

Past tense? 'And now?'

'Now it's going to be even harder keeping things professional.'

'Back in London?' Back in the real world. Where adrenaline-fuelled kisses and dramatic sunsets didn't happen.

'It would be inappropriate for me to start something with you.'

'Inappropriate?' She sat up and tucked her knees to her chest. How politically correct.

He followed her upright. 'I'm the manager of the station running your promotion. I sign the cheques that pay for your classes.'

And would do for months yet.

'And it's not fair to you, either. You're not equipped for something like this.'

She sat back, hard. Shook her head. 'Like what?'

'Something happening between us.'

*Not everyone's cut out for seduction*, he'd joked back at spy school, though maybe it hadn't been entirely a joke. She had failed abysmally at flirting her way to information from a stranger in class, though Zander's eyes had remained glued to her the whole time. But that was…you know…a stranger. And this was Zander.

Totally different situation.

Though maybe not for him. How cruel to kiss her half to

death, to make her feel so desirable, and then to back-pedal so very obviously.

He rambled on. 'This was—'

*Fantastic? Overdue?*

'—an aberration.'

Pain sliced through her. Could he have found an uglier way of saying it was a mistake? She stared across at Scotland, and would have given anything to spontaneously teleport over to the far bank.

'I should have had more control,' he said. 'This is my fault.'

*Oh, please.* 'I came up here willingly.'

'Not expecting that, I'm sure.'

No. Definitely not expecting that. She just wanted to get to know him a little bit. But she'd discovered a whole other Zander hidden inside the first one. 'So now what? We just go back to how it was?'

He looked at her.

Did he need it spelled out? 'You ignoring me?'

'I won't ignore you, George. I couldn't, now.'

*George.* The same nickname her friends used for her. The irony bit hard. 'So then business as usual?'

Silence was nod enough.

She pushed to her feet. 'OK, then. Well, my first order of business is to get back to London before dawn.'

'I'm staying at the Arms. Maybe they'll have a second room?'

Was he joking? Stay anywhere near him and not want to be with him? While he found her so...ill-equipped?

'I have a prep session for the personal makeover tomorrow morning. Measuring and stuff.' Never mind that she'd never felt less like doing anything. Despite—apparently—needing all the help she could get. She grasped her excuses as she found them.

'I'll walk you to your car,' Zander said.

For a guy who had protested so vehemently about her catching the underground home after a couple of wines, he was sure very willing to let her drive a deadly weapon half way across the country with still-scattered wits.

Maybe he wanted her gone as much as she needed to be there?

They walked, in silence, back up the road to her vehicle. The rapid journey from body-against-body and lips-against-lips to this awful, careful distance was jarring, but the cold night breeze helped her to blow the final wisps of desire from her mind like fog from shore.

It was for the better. Almost certainly.

She turned and faced him, a bright smile on her face. 'See you Wednesday night, then?'

Salsa class.

She held her breath. If he was going to pull out of his pledge to go with her, now was the moment it would happen.

He stared down at her, leaned forward as if to kiss her again, but pulled on the handle of the car door behind her instead. 'See you Wednesday.'

Him being chivalrous with the door went exactly no way to making her feel any better about what an ass he'd just been back on the bank of the firth. She grunted her thanks, slipped into her front seat, and slammed the door shut on his parting words.

*Drive safely.*

# CHAPTER SEVEN

THE best run of his life turned into the worst night of his life.

Not the evening—the evening touched on one of the most special moments he'd ever had. But the night, after Georgia drove off so quickly down Bowness's quiet main street… He barely slept that night despite his exhaustion and even Sunday was pretty much a write-off.

He spent the whole time trying to offload the kiss he had stolen from her like a fence trying to move appropriated diamonds. Failing abysmally.

After all these months—even after the stern talking to he'd given himself after getting all touchy feely with her at spy school—why had he let himself slip to quite that degree?

Kissing her. Touching her.

Torturing himself with what he couldn't have.

There were endless numbers of women back in London that he could kiss. And touch. And sleep with if he wanted. Bold, casual, riskless women. Georgia Stone was not one of them. She wasn't made of the same stuff as any of them. She wasn't bold or casual. And Lord knew not without risk.

But then she'd walked into his world, the only woman—the only person—ever to watch him race, to wait with a cold drink and a proud smile at the finish line, and he'd let himself buy into the fantasy. Just for a moment. Then one fantasy had led to another until they were lying in the long, cool grass, tongues and feet tangling.

He'd let himself slip further than any time since Lara.

Worse, to *trust*. And he didn't do trust.

Ever.

He'd finally tumbled into an exhausted sleep Sunday night, but his mood was no better today.

As evidenced by the way his staff were tiptoeing around him extra carefully. Even Casey, who usually only gave the most cursory of knocks before walking into his office, actually stood, waiting, until he gave her permission to enter.

'Zander,' she started, lips tight. She looked as if she'd rather be calling him Mr Rush.

'What is it, Casey?'

'I wanted to…' She changed tack. 'Georgia just emailed these instructions, and I thought I'd better run them past you.'

That got his attention. Not just because the sentence had the word *Georgia* in it, but because his assistant and their resident scientist were thick as thieves, so Casey ratting her out meant something big was going on.

She stood across the desk from him. 'She's made some changes to the programme.'

No big news—Georgia changed things around regularly. He was getting used to it. He stared and waited for more from Casey.

'Big changes.' She held out a sheaf of papers.

'How big?' But as he ran his eyes over them he could see instantly. 'Ankara? Are you kidding me?' He eyeballed his assistant. She took half a step back. 'Ibiza's already booked isn't it?' Their flights to Spain were in a few weeks. Georgia's big holiday. Now she wanted it to be Turkey?

'Actually I can still make changes—'

Not what he wanted to hear.

Casey's mouth clicked shut. She started backing out of the room. 'I'll leave you to read the—'

'Stay!' he barked, though deep down he regretted commanding her like a trained dog. None of this was her fault.

All of it was his. He'd been stupid to give into his baser instincts and kiss her. As though either of them could go back from that.

He flipped to the next page. Georgia had ditched the cocktail-making class in favour of life drawing. She'd dumped aquasphering on the Thames to go on some underground tour of old London. She'd dropped out of salsa and replaced it with belly dancing, for heaven's sake.

'I see spy lessons made the cut,' he snorted.

'Yeah, she loves those—' Again, Casey's jaw clicked shut. As if she suddenly realised she was siding with the enemy.

'Get her on the phone for me.'

'I tried, Zander. She's not answering.'

Right. 'I'll take care of it tonight.' At salsa.

Assuming she went at all.


'I wasn't convinced you'd be here,' he said as Georgia slipped through the dance studio door, quietly, and joined him on the benches. She smiled and nodded at some of their fellow dance regulars. Twice as big as the paltry smile she'd offered him.

'I wasn't sure if the change got approved, so I didn't want to leave them with uneven numbers.'

'What's with the swap to belly dancing?'

She shrugged and glanced around the room. Zander tried again. 'I had no idea you were such a fan of all things eastern. First belly dancing, then Ankara…'

She brought her eyes back to his. Surprised at his snark, perhaps. 'You helped me to see that my list was built out of things I thought I should be doing more than things I actually wanted to do.'

'Come on, Georgia. You actually want to belly dance?'

She kicked her chin up. He might as well have waved a red flag. 'It interests me. It's beautiful.'

*Uh-huh.* It couldn't have anything to do with the fact that belly dancing was a solo occupation and she wouldn't have to touch him again. 'And what's in Ankara that's of so much more interest than Ibiza?'

Other than less alcohol, less noise, less crowds.

'Cappadocia.'

'And what's that?'

'A region full of amazing remnants of a Bronze-Aged civilisation. You can fly over it in balloons.'

He just stared. 'And that's what you want to do?'

Her hands crept up to her hips. 'Yes.'

'Why the sudden change of heart on all your activities?'

'It's not all that sudden. I don't want expensive makeovers or hot stone massages or guidance on how to wear clothes I'll never be able to afford to buy.'

The dance instructor clapped them to attention.

'Is this about the cost?' Zander whispered furiously. Hoping it really was.

'This is about me. Doing things that matter to me.'

It was her money—her year—to spend however she liked. And it was his job to make even the wackiest list sound like something all EROS' listeners could relate to. But it was becoming increasingly important that it helped Georgia to find her way back to feeling whole. He wanted her whole.

He just didn't know why.

'Partners!' the dance instructor called.

They knew the drill. They'd done weeks of this. He'd gone a little bit crazy getting all the audio he needed, grabs from Georgia, the dance instructor. That should have been heaps. But he'd interviewed just about everyone else, there, too. Every single one of them had an interesting story, their own personal reasons for learning to dance at seventy, or despite being widowed recently or coming alone. And for every single one of them it wasn't about dance at all.

It was about living.

There were thirty interesting stories in this room. But he was only paid to tell one of them.

The instructor clapped his hands again. He and Georgia were supposed to partner up. She was supposed to step into his arms, assume the salsa start position. But the stance they were supposed to assume was the vertical version of the one they'd found themselves in a few nights ago: lying there in the long grass as the sun extinguished in the ocean.

A little bit too familiar.

A little bit too real.

She hovered indecisively. And again, this was his mess to sort out. He was the one who'd failed to control his wandering thoughts and hands that night. He was the one who'd lacked discipline. Folded to his barely acknowledged need for human contact.

He stepped closer to her, kept his body as formal and stiff as he could. Raised his hands. 'Georgia…?'

Her smile was tight, but she stepped into his hold carefully, and stood—just as stiff, just as formal—close to his body. As the music began he did his best not to brush against her unless essential—out of respect for her and a general aversion to self-torture—and they stepped as they'd been taught, though nowhere near as fluid as it had been in the past.

It was as clunky as them, together, now.

But it was functional.

The instructor drifted around correcting posture, demonstrating steps, voicing words of encouragement, but when he got to the two of them he took one look at their total disconnect, his lips pursed and he said in his thick accent, 'Not every day is magic. Sometimes this happens. You will have the magic again next week.'

No. There would be no magic next week. There would be no salsa next week. And the guilt in Georgia's eyes confirmed exactly what he'd suspected. This sudden change to belly dancing was about *him*.

'I could have just stopped coming,' he gritted as she moved close enough to hear his murmur.

She drifted away again. But he knew the steps would bring her right back. He tried to read her face and see if she was going to feign innocence or not.

'I wanted something that didn't force us to dance together,' she breathed, her total honesty pleasing him on some deep level. A level deep beneath the one where he hated what she was suggesting. 'The only other solo option was pole dancing. Belly dancing seemed like a decent compromise.'

And suddenly his mind was filled with poles and Georgia and seedy, darkened venues. He forced his focus back onto the key issue.

'What about the segment?'

'You've got more than enough for a salsa segment. In fact, why do you have so much? You'll never use all of that in a two-minute piece.'

Prime-time air was too expensive to dedicate more than two minutes a month to the Year of Georgia. So why had he spent all that time recording everyone else in the session as well? 'The laws of documentary-making,' he hedged. 'Get ten times more than you think you'll need.'

'This isn't a documentary,' she reminded him, her breath coming faster with the dancing. 'It's a stupid commercial promotion.'

*Stupid.* Nice.

But he was too distracted remembering the last time she'd been this breathless to argue.

He yanked her towards him as the funky music crescendoed. As usual the whole room was slightly out of synch so what was supposed to be a passionate crash of body against body always looked like a vaguely geriatric Mexican wave.

She pressed against his chest, staring up at him, angry colour staining her cheeks. 'I've changed my mind.'

'About what?'

'My reluctance to have a stranger come along with me. You can go back to your paperwork and give me the work-experience kid as far as I'm concerned.'

'You think our schedules are that elastic? That I can just make a change like that with no warning? Disrupt everyone's plans every time you change your mind?'

'It's called dynamism, Zander,' she gritted. 'Maybe your station could use some.'

OK, now she was just picking a fight.

He stopped when he should have twirled her into open position. She stumbled at his misstep. Then he curled his hand around hers and hauled her back towards the door. A few eyes followed them, including the speculative ones of the instructor.

'Next week!' he shouted at their backs. 'Magic!'

She shook free as soon as they hit the cool June air. 'What are you doing?'

'What's going on, Georgia?'

'Nothing's going on. I just realised that I needed to be true to myself or this whole thing is a crock.'

'Which part is being true to yourself? The part where you start switching all our plans around or the part where you'll do just about anything not to get too close to me.'

*'Aberration,'* she parroted back to him. 'That was your word, Zander. You wanted things back on a professional footing.'

'Not at the expense of any civility at all between us.'

Her breath hissed out of her. 'The changes I'm making are trying to keep things civil. So they don't end up like this every night.'

Boundaries. She was stacking them up and he kept knocking them down. Why? He should be thanking her. He took two deep, long breaths. 'We just kissed, Georgia. Heat of the moment, influence of the sunset, romance of the wall. Whatever you want to call it.'

He had to call it something, otherwise he was just a jerk for hitting on her while she was still vulnerable from her breakup with Bradford.

'Who are you trying to convince, Zander? Me or yourself?'

That was a damned fine question. 'It doesn't have to change anything. We just agree to let it go.'

'Just like that?'

Sure. He was a master at denial. 'I have a job to do and you have money to spend. Let's just focus on that.'

'You don't object to any of the changes?'

'I don't care what you do with the money, I just want you to be—' he caught himself a half-breath before saying *happy* '—comfortable with it.'

'I'm hoping I'll be more comfortable this way. Forcing myself to do things way outside of my usual interests was probably a mistake. I was trying to be someone I'm not.'

'Why?'

'Because I thought it was what was expected. What your listeners would expect. What you wanted.'

Her eyes flicked away and he struggled with the deep satisfaction that she'd done any of it for him. 'Listeners are the first to spot falsity on air. If it's not of interest to you it's going to show in the segments.'

She nodded. 'Well, hopefully we've taken care of that now.'

*We.* He liked her accidental use of the collective. For the same reason he liked coming along to these crazy classes even though he had much more efficient things to be doing with that time. It legitimised his being with Georgia. He could play at relationships without actually being in one. Enjoy her company without the commitment. She was generous with her wonder and excitement doing new things and he could live off that for a whole week back in the soul-destroying environment of the station.

If he spaced it out right.

Kisses… Those he could live off for a year.

She chewed her lip. 'Should we go back in?'

Her reasons for changing classes were valid. The more he had to put his hands on her, the harder it was going to be taking them off. 'No. Let's just call it a night.'

'Sure.'

Courteous but cool. It bothered him enough to glance down the street for the nearest coffee shop. He saw the blinking LED sign a few blocks down. So much safer than having her in his house. So much safer than a bar with a few drinks under his belt. So much safer than the back of a black taxi, pressed together for twenty minutes.

'Let's grab a coffee,' he said and turned her west.

Georgia did her best not to flinch at the feel of Zander's hand at her lower back. It was just a courteous gesture. Unconscious. It didn't mean a thing. Even if it did feel more intimate and personal than the salsa clinch they'd been in just moments before. Something about the way it failed to entirely disengage even once she was fully moving...

It took a few silent minutes to get to the Tudor-style coffee shop. Then a few more to get seated and settled and their drinks ordered.

She struggled to not be distracted by his long fingers tapping on the tabletop—fingers that had traced her skin so beautifully just nights ago and curled so strongly in her hair. But if she looked at his face she'd either drown in his eyes or start obsessing about his lips.

All of which were entirely off limits to her now. Despite the torment of the taste-test after the marathon.

So she fluctuated between looking at the place where a lock of his hair fell across his forehead, a spot of fluff on his collar and glancing around the room at the other patrons.

'Tell me about Ankara.'

That managed to bring her eyes back to his. 'Now?'

'I know nothing about it and I'm going to be going with you. Why is it so special?'

'Cappadocia.' Amongst other wonders.

He shrugged. 'Old cities and ballooning. That's it?'

She pressed forwards against the table. 'Seriously? You can't understand why someone would want to float high above a city where houses and chapels are carved into the rockfaces? Where entire communities used to live underground to hide from invaders two thousand years ago? Cities that were founded twenty centuries before Jesus?'

He just stared. 'You're serious?'

Excited warmth warmed her cheeks. 'Where else could you do it? It's so intriguing…'

'It's not to put me off?'

'It's not about you at all.' *Lies!* 'It's something I'd like to do. I saw it in a documentary years ago and I've never forgotten it.' And if Zander came along, bonus. Good things happened to them when they got out of London. Things just tended to go south when they were back in it.

His eyes burned into hers. Deciding. He slid his recorder up onto the table. 'OK. Tell me more.'

She did. For the next hour and a half. All about Göreme, where she wanted to stay, all about Cappadocia's extraordinary ancient lunar-scapes and traditional villages and the amazing peoples that had lived there for forty centuries. All about how it had wheedled its way under her skin all those years ago.

'And you can stay in these underground buildings?'

'They carve them out of the side of enormous rock faces. And they've been modernised. Electricity, water. They even have Wi-Fi. So you won't be slumming it.'

He'd been smiling for the last five or six minutes straight, though she knew she wasn't saying anything funny. His eyes practically glittered looking at her.

'What?'

'You just…' He struggled for the right words. And he turned the recorder off. 'You *love* life, don't you?'

Generally, she just endured life. But maybe that was be-cause she'd been missing the best of it. 'I love the possibilities.

I love that you've given me this opportunity and I'm going to do something I've always wanted to. I couldn't do this without you.'

'Without the station,' he clarified.

*Right.* Just in case she was thinking he was doing this for *her.* 'Without help.'

'You might have got there by yourself. Eventually.'

'Maybe not. I was this close—' she pinched her fingers '—to consigning myself to the role of wife and mother. That would have meant a lot less flexibility and freedom for a really long time.'

He shrugged. 'A different kind of adventure, perhaps?'

His words sank in. If marriage was an adventure, then shouldn't you enter into it with someone that you'd want to be adventurous with? Discover new worlds with? Fly across a lunar landscape with. Her breath tightened up. She said the first thing that came into her head in order to stop anything more inappropriate appearing there.

'Is that what you think marriage is? An adventure?'

'I used to.' He pressed his lips together the moment those few tiny words voiced.

The unexpected glimpse into his past was tantalising. She wanted more immediately. 'Is that why you created the Valentine's promo?' she fished. 'To celebrate marriage?'

His answer was fifty-per-cent snort. 'Definitely not. I created the promo to cash in on the leap year commercialisation. Nothing more.'

Well, that was depressingly cynical. 'You don't think matrimony is worth celebrating?'

'On the whole I think marriage is highly overrated.'

She stared at him. 'I guess that shouldn't surprise me. Otherwise you'd have been snapped up ages ago.'

One expressive eyebrow lifted. 'You don't think I'd have done the snapping?'

'You strike me as a man who gets what he wants. If you

wanted a wife in that big lonely house of yours there'd be one there now.'

He drained the last of his second coffee. 'You have a very high opinion of my desirability. Not everyone would agree with you.'

His staff perhaps? 'Maybe you work too hard keeping people at a distance...'

'You're here.' He tossed it out like a challenge. 'I can't seem to shake you at all.'

His light words filleted her neatly along her ribs. Although, she could see he wasn't saying them to be cruel. In fact, if anything, he looked more engaged and more intent than ever. And positively mystified.

'I'm particularly uncaring about societal niceties,' she murmured. 'I'm sure there's been a hundred not-so-subtle hints I should have been taking.'

If she weren't so busy looking for hints that he might be more interested than he was letting on. Maybe than he even knew, himself. But for every sultry look, for every gentle touch, for every unexpected waterside kiss there was a frown, pressed lips, words like *professional* and *aberration*. And *ill-equipped*.

They kind of cancelled each other out.

'Besides,' she braved on, 'I'm not your target market.'

His eyes narrowed. 'Really? Who is?'

She looked around. A lone woman sat reading a thick book in the far corner. Her perfectly manicured nails were the exact same shade as her shoes. 'Her. Maybe...' She looked around for someone else. 'Maybe her?'

Two glamour queens in one coffee shop. Convenient.

Zander looked around far more subtly than she had. 'They're both very attractive.'

Of course that would be the first thing he noticed.

'And stylish,' he went on.

'And well educated.' She nodded to the woman with the thick hardback. 'She's reading Ayn Rand.'

'And that's who you think my target market is? Stylish intellectuals?'

'I can see either one of them in your house very easily.' Much as it galled her to admit it.

His grey eyes pierced her. 'Can you see them sitting on the side of a weather-beaten old track for an hour making conversation with the locals while waiting to hand me an energy drink?'

She just stared. Because, no, she couldn't.

'So maybe my target market isn't as clear-cut as you think?' His chin rested on his steepled fingers and he lifted it enough to tilt his head.

*Maybe not.*

'It's a moot point, anyway,' she breezed. 'If you're not actually *in* the market.'

He started to answer that but then changed his mind. His mouth gently closed again without making a sound.

'So three weeks before the underground cities?' he hedged, after a moment.

'And two dance classes before then.'

'What about my garden?'

She studied him. This man was more baffling than any of the complex scientific mysteries she'd studied at university. His garden had sat there, untouched, for years. Now suddenly he wanted it to progress immediately? 'What about it?'

'Don't you want to see how it's progressing?'

Did she want to see what some other lucky sod got to create with? 'When it's done.'

It was never too late to implement some self-restraint.

That triggered a couple of lines between his brows. 'Guess I should trade in my dancing shoes and get onto a visa for Turkey, then.'

'Ten minutes and ten pounds at Heathrow.' She nodded. 'I checked.'

He considered her. Then smiled. 'You're really excited.'

There was something looming on her horizon and every

cell in her body told her it had something to do with Turkey. It had been swaying her away from Ibiza almost the moment she agreed to Spain. Making her look east. Agitating subconsciously for her to change her mind. And then, the moment she'd made her decision, this odd kind of emotional hum had commenced and it had been slowly building ever since.

Ankara. Cappadocia.

Something was going to happen there. Something life-changing. Something that felt almost fated. Briefly she wondered how she ever would have found her way there if not for the disaster that was her botched proposal, if she hadn't met Dan before that. And suddenly everything started to feel very...

Meant.

*Excited?* About standing on the edge of something so huge and new?

'You have no idea,' she breathed.

Georgia stood at the door to the curtained-off change area in the dance studio and hovered awkwardly in the doorway. Possibly she hadn't thought this through as thoroughly as she might have.

Imagine that.

'Off you go...' the woman behind her nudged. Emma. A friendly, motherly sort. A total born-again about belly dancing, given she'd only been coming a few weeks herself.

Georgia took a deep breath to quell her nerves. Maybe belly dancing wasn't the best choice to get away from the close body contact with Zander, the brushing and heated touching. Salsa was, at least, a partnered thing. It wasn't Zander sitting on a seat in the corner watching her wiggle and jiggle and cavort around semi-naked.

Even if it was very prettily semi-naked.

Turned out one of the things this class loved the best was a newcomer. A newcomer who turned up in the middle of a semester and in a tracksuit. The lesson of the day went on hold and all the women helped rifle through the dress-up box of spare belly-dancing bits to put a full costume together—educating her the whole time about each piece's name, purpose, and heritage—then they thrust them at Georgia and thrust her into the change room.

Zander sent his digital recorder in with one of the ladies to capture the sounds of the excited chaos and was cooling his heels out in the dance area, getting the necessary permission forms all ready for their return.

Georgia glanced in the mirror. Her full, beaded skirt fell from her hips down to brush the floor and the matching top-piece they'd selected for her was equally modest—no worse than the vest tops she often wore at home in summer—cupping her small breasts and cascading stringed coins down in a V to point at her exposed belly button. She'd never before mourned her slim build—in fact her curvier friends had envied her for it—but standing here amongst the luscious curves and generous breasts and gorgeous outfits of the other women in the class she'd never wished more to be curvier. Rounded instead of flat.

And Zander was about to get an eyeful of all that flatness.

Emma pinned Georgia's face veil up behind her ear and gave her a shove.

'Out you go, love. Get it over with.'

Then they all rushed out, ankle bells ringing, dragging her along in their bright, jangly wake.

Zander's eyes locked on her the moment she stepped out. How he spotted her amongst so many disguised, Technicolor women was a mystery. Unless he was just looking for the only boyish figure in the room.

She shrivelled up inside, instantly. This had to be her most foolish of fool-moments…

The woman he'd given his digital recorder to returned it to him with a flirty smile, and he flirted right back. In fact, from that moment on he seemed to become entranced by every other woman in the room and—God love them—they enjoyed his presence just as much. Far from being shy about the presence of a strange man in this heavily female environment, the room full of housewives, teachers, and bank clerks dressed in little more than sexy pyjamas lapped it up, escaping into their dance personas and focusing their attention on the only man in the room.

They weren't gratuitous—they seemed respectful of the awkwardness of Zander's position—but they were thorough. They zeroed their efforts on him and unleashed the full force of the moves for his benefit.

He grinned his way through the whole thing.

But avoided looking at her at all.

Small mercy, perhaps, given how hot she flamed and how stumbling her movements were. But she'd signed up here for a reason—actually two reasons—and she wasn't in a hurry to go back to the close, breathy, partnered clinch of salsa nor to be doomed for ever to being *not cut out for seduction.*

She lifted her chin, willing to bet that every woman in this room turned up in a tracksuit the first time and had to ease their way into the rhythmic gyrations they were currently exorcising on an indulgent Zander. And every one of them must have felt exactly as out of place and outclassed as she now did.

But had they ever felt as invisible? Despite the raunchy outfit?

Or was she deluded in thinking the draped fabrics and accenting jewels were attractive? Maybe where she saw rich, sensual colour, he saw tacky, flashy glitz.

She turned back for the change rooms.

'Not yet, love,' the instructor called, leaving Zander to fend for himself against the barrage of oestrogen and turning Georgia away from the gaggle that shielded her from his *non*-gaze towards the large mirrors lining the wall.

She forced her focus on the instructor, keeping one eye on the professional moves and the other on her own reflection, mimicking the basic choreography, taking correction, and trying to repeat the positions and sequences of the more experienced dancers.

Keeping her eyes steadfastly off the man in the background the whole time.

Belly dancing wasn't about sex, the instructor told her, correcting Georgia's too-jerky hips. It was about empowerment. But right now she felt pretty darned sexy. And that wasn't something she could remember feeling in the past.

Pleasure, sure. But not sexy. Not…sensual.

The fluidity of the moves started to come more naturally, and the way the soft fabric brushing against her bare skin accentuated and teased her senses. It made her feel so…alive.

Between the concentration, the keeping of her arms above her head, and the surprising amount of effort required to gyrate everything that needed to be gyrating, her colour and her breath were up in no time. And with rows of dancers between her and the only distraction in the room she was able to concentrate better, forcing the embarrassment away with her focus and determination. It took no time at all to realise that every woman here wore a mask, something they slipped on with the beautiful fabrics. She might not be naturally seductive but, by God, she'd learn to fake it. Under her veil, she could be anyone she wanted. Sexier, smarter, stronger, more fun, more delightful—everything Zander and Kelly and Dan and her mother thought she apparently should be.

She twisted and twirled and undulated to the throng of the music and kept her eyes firmly locked on her own reflection in the mirror. She took a few more risks. She turned and twirled and kept only half an eye on what Zander was doing as he wandered the room, recording the music and the vocalisations of the women who danced for—and around—him.

He seemed totally uninterested in her presence.

Anger fuelled her moves, turned them more defiant.

*Really, Zander? Even this isn't enough…?*

She spun back to the mirror, tired of trying to be what other people wanted and failing. Tired of making her decisions based on priorities that weren't her own. She was going to be wild and sexy and beautiful just because she could. Here, in this place and in these clothes, she could.

Zander could go jump.

She slowly raised already-aching arms above her head, her concentration focused on the serpentine movements of her hands, the slow twists, the way the dozens of borrowed bracelets jangled and spun on her undulating wrists. She swayed and rolled and let her head fall back, her eyes close, and just felt the music, felt the movement of the women around her.

And she danced purely for the pleasure of it.

And then she lowered her gaze back to the mirror, back to her own flushed reflection and sparkling eyes.

Straight into Zander's.

Everyone else in the room danced on, the instructor dissolved tactfully back into the throng and the odd person danced across the gap between them. But it did nothing to shake Georgia's gaze free of Zander's.

Every part of *old* Georgia screamed to stop. Still. On the spot.

Yet her body kept moving. Fluid, teasing. Flirting.

And just like that she felt the empowerment kick in.

Two hours ago she wouldn't have been able to brush up against him without feeling self-conscious, but behind the veil she could do anything. Be anyone. She could look at him as she'd so desperately been wanting.

She danced on. His recorder hung, ignored, by his side.

Around them, the music faded slowly, the chat-level rose. A door opened on the far side and someone's husband tiptoed in with a small boy in tow, both of them dressed in football colours. The balance between make-believe and real-world started to shift back.

Georgia lowered her arms, and her eyes. And she turned.

Zander still watched her, though his own expression was as guarded as hers must have been.

'That was fun,' she said, still breathing out the exertion. Not ready to lose the rush of empowerment.

He looked around them. A few covert glances looked back. 'For everyone, it seems.'

'Great workout.' But all that did was draw his eyes to the heaving rise and fall of her tiny, beaded top. And he didn't speak, just nodded his agreement.

'I'll just get changed. Won't be a minute.' She knew what came next. He always liked to interview her right after the first class, to capture her first impressions. She wasn't sufficiently clothed or her breath sufficiently recovered to do that just yet. She followed a couple of other women into the change area. Most went home exactly as they were so it was just the few of them, all newer participants, returning to street wear.

They chatted excitedly as they stripped off the layers of magic and mystery and slid themselves back into their clothes. Just one hour ago being in her underwear in front of strangers was excruciating. Now they were sisters. Lumps, bumps, big, small. The thing that had shifted inside her wasn't switching back.

The three others had only been coming weeks and were curious whether she'd enjoyed it, whether she'd be back. She knew, without question, that she would.

'I hope you're bringing *him* every week,' Emma said. 'Way to change the dynamic!'

They all laughed.

'No one means any offence by dancing for your man,' another said. 'It's just the novelty.'

'He's not my man,' Georgia was fast to correct, though low so that Zander wouldn't hear them through the flimsy fabric walls.

That caused more hilarity. 'Oh, love,' Emma whispered, 'if he's not I think he soon will be. We all saw his face while you were dancing. He's wound as tight as a drum. It would be a shame if no one was to benefit from all our good work tonight.'

Georgia stopped one leg halfway into her tracksuit bottoms and stared at the women. They laughed wildly again. She understood exactly. A weird kind of adrenaline was still coursing through her body, too. She would have joined their laughter if the suggestion hadn't thrown her into such a breathless stupor. And an unshakeable vision of her *benefitting* from tonight's endeavours.

She tidied her hair, carefully folded her borrowed costume items, and placed them in the washing pile, and then dawdled a moment longer. Delaying the inevitable. She wasn't sure she could walk out there and see Zander if the women with all their speculation were still around.

The longer she took, the fewer people would be in the room.

But eventually she couldn't delay any longer. He needed his interview. She rolled the waistband of her running pants down to be more like the beautiful women she saw at the gym, more like the low-hung skirt that had just caressed her legs. More casual. As if this weren't an enormous deal. She took a deep breath and stepped out of the change area into the dance space. Only a handful lingered. None of them was male. After the events of the evening she couldn't really blame Zander for stepping outside so that he didn't have to face his unexpected seductresses in the full fluorescent light of indoors.

She thanked the instructor warmly and whole-heartedly, assured her she would be back the following week and stepped out into the cool night air.

She looked left.

She looked right.

She looked across the road in case he was leaning on the lamppost, waiting.

Her stomach clenched. Nothing. No Zander anywhere.

They'd arrived separately but she saw him pull up so she knew where his Jag was. Tucking her crossed hands under her armpits, she hurried down the road a way in case he was waiting in his car. But there was just a dry rectangle on the otherwise rain-dampened road where his Jag had been.

Gone.

Her jaw tightened. Maybe he'd gone for a drink with one of the other participants in the class. Maybe he'd formed a connection with someone in particular while she was so busy ignoring how he was ignoring her. But that seemed both unlikely and unfair to Zander—he wasn't a complete jerk. His absence didn't automatically mean he'd scarpered with some hot, bejewelled stranger. It just meant he hadn't stayed to see her.

That probably should have made her feel better.

But it didn't.

All that power, the erotic blast, the sensual costume…the out and out *risk* she'd taken forcing herself to let those secret feelings show on the outside. All that had done was sent Zander running. So embarrassed by her display that he couldn't even stick around to face her.

She'd thought maybe he was being tactful, keeping his eyes averted, trying to make a difficult class that bit easier for her. That maybe he was more affected than he was letting on. She'd thought that burning, blazing moment in the mirror might have been sensual desire pumping back at her.

But what if it was anger? Or discomfort.

A tight ball settled high in her chest. Maybe he was just plain embarrassed. Just because he'd admitted to there being some chemistry between them didn't mean he wanted it there. Or wanted to do anything about it beyond the kiss they'd shared—some lousy accident of adrenaline.

She hooked her thumbs under the curled waist of her pants and let them unravel back to their usually modest position. She flattened them down with unsteady fingers as deep sorrow washed through her.

That was it.

She was done.

If who she was just wasn't enough for the high standards of Alekzander Rush, then so be it. She liked Georgia Stone. Lots of people did. And not because she was a carbon copy of everyone else spilling out of London's entertainment district, but because she was *her*: loyal and bookish and fond of long, quiet walks in ancient forests and lazy afternoons with girlfriends tucking into a steaming ale pie.

She'd set out on the Year of Georgia to find out who she really was and—surprise, surprise—she'd been there all along. And it only took her half a year.

She turned and walked the block back to her car.

And if Zander didn't like the Georgia she'd uncovered, well...his loss.

# CHAPTER EIGHT

*August*

THERE really weren't enough showers cold enough or long
enough to get the haunting, hot mirror scene out of Zander's
mind. It was all too easy to cop out when you were the boss,
when you had staff to do things for you.

*Minions.*

He'd never felt the distinction so clearly until he had Casey
ring Georgia up and let her know he wouldn't be coming to
belly-dancing classes with her any more. That she was OK to
go to them solo. That he got what he needed that first night.
It wasn't hard to find an excuse. Salsa was on a Wednesday
night. Belly dancing was on a Tuesday. He had network meetings until late on a Tuesday.

Not so late that he couldn't get across town to the dance
studio, in fact, but it was too convenient an excuse to pass up.
There was no way on this green earth that he was setting foot
back in there while Georgia was around.

He'd already been back to see the instructor, to get from
her the interview he'd been too much of a coward to get from
Georgia right after her first class had finished. It was only the
fact that her borrowed car was parked virtually outside the
door to the dance studio that made it even remotely OK that
he'd just bolted on her. Left her there alone.

What a class act.

She hadn't called him on it. Or emailed. Or even asked Casey what was up with her coward of a boss. And that said a lot about how she was feeling about his disappearing act. Defiant. Irritated.

Possibly hurt.

But getting hands-on with her was no better an idea now than it had been up at Hadrian's Wall. And so walking out of there seemed like the most prudent action at the time. He'd spent a lot of time and energy avoiding emotional entanglements, focusing on his career; this was really no different. If spending time around Georgia was making it too hard to keep her at arm's length, then there was really only one solution.

Getting Casey to do his dirty work for him—well, there was no excuse for that. He'd just needed some space from the mirror scene before they headed off into the wilds of Turkey together.

But that was only effective if he could exorcise the memory branded into his brain.

And three hours in the air and three more in a car—no matter how luxurious—was a lot of nothing to try and fill with other thoughts.

Another cowardly act. Getting Casey to shift his flights so that they weren't travelling together. That bought him precious more hours to build up his reserves against Georgia. To get through the weekend in Turkey. Both of them had jobs to be back for come Monday morning so this was the most fleeting of Turkish experiences. But he'd re-routed through Istanbul whereas Georgia was touching down in Ankara. Again, precious hours for last-minute fortification.

'Göreme.'

His driver slowed on the limits of a village. At first glance it looked much like the extraordinary landscape they'd been driving through for some time: gorgeous, golden rock faces, enormous jutting spurs of sandstone. But as they got closer Zander started to notice the details. Square edges, dark windows, balconies, a layer-cake of dwellings carved into the rock face. They drove more fully into town and it looked much like any other, people milling around stone storefronts with brightly painted signs on them, cars angle-parked in front for the convenience of shoppers. But behind it—towering high behind it—a rock face filled with homes.

And hotels. Like the one he was heading for.

They pulled around a corner and the whole city unfolded before him. A mix of enormous stone monoliths surrounded by carved homes. And nearly a dozen bright colourful balloons drifting silently overhead. The sharp protrusions of the rocks contrasted with the square edges of the façades of the cave-houses and the bulbous curves of the hot-air balloons, which dropped insanely low to give their passengers a good look at one of Cappadocia's underground cities.

The whole thing was bathed in a golden, afternoon light.

Zander wound his window down and breathed in the air— sweet, fresh and carrying a distinctive tang. Was it apples?

He asked his driver.

'Shisha,' he said simply. The apple-flavoured tobacco smoked by the locals.

The car stopped in front of a stone hotel that reflected the shapes of the entire city. Square edges of the block construction of the fascia of the hotel, the rolling curves of the darkened archways that led deep into the rock face, and the sharp, zig-zagging stairways that led up the mountain face to the dwellings higher up. But the closer he looked, the more detail he saw.

Intricate carved patterns around the doors and windows. Niches everywhere filled with bright intriguing ornaments, and potted colour spilling from every available surface.

Clearly the Cappadocians loved their plants as much as Georgia did.

Georgia.

He looked up the length of the building, at some of the balconies carved into the rock face, as if she'd be standing there waiting for him. A beautiful smile on her face. Bouncing on her toes the way she did when she got excited.

He forced the image away. That kind of thinking was barred, too.

It took a few minutes to register in the small, cool interior of the hotel reception. From where he stood he could see five possible exits. A set of stairs going up, another set twisting Escher-style around to the left and down, a small archway and a larger one to its right and the view behind him after his climb to the hotel's entrance. A balcony wall dotted with pot plants and with an old shingled sign saying *Reception*. A ginger kitten rubbed its cheek contentedly on the sign while another slept curled around the base of the plant in the pot. And behind them, the extraordinary expanse of the city.

'This is amazing,' he murmured to himself.

'Welcome to Göreme,' the young girl said in confident English. Better than his driver's. And certainly better than his own Turkish. 'This way.'

He followed her through the labyrinthine interior of the hotel, instantly feeling the heat of the desert afternoon drop off as the earth's insulation did its job. The walls, windows and stairs of the hotel were all carved from the surrounding mountain.

'I hope you will be comfortable here,' the girl said, pausing at a landing with a timber door. She pushed it open. The room inside was enormous and open-plan. Carved entirely out of the ancient limestone, its walls streaked with eons of stratification. On one side, a large window faced the bobbing hot-air balloons outside, streaming golden light in from the west.

Polished timber floors stretched out underfoot and carved archways led off in two directions. One to an external balcony niche and one to the natural flagstone floor of a luxury bathroom deeper in the rock face. The whole place was filled with plump, bright furniture, and traditional rugs and light fixtures.

*Comfortable?* 'I can't see how I could be anything but.'

Truly the most amazing thing he'd ever seen.

He thanked the girl and closed the door after her, then set about exploring, following his nose to a new extraordinary smell. His balcony had its own large niche built into it off to the side of his room. Off the side of the rockface. It had an expansive daybed complete with rich linens and a small, low circular fire on the stone floor, on which hot Turkish coffee bubbled away on a piece of roasting hot slate. A ubiquitous hookah was set up ready to go next to it preloaded with fragrant tobacco.

He poured himself a cup of dark, strong coffee immediately. Then he turned and stared at the view down to the hustle and bustle a dozen flights of steps below and out across the valley of houses to the ones lining the hill on the other side.

All so ancient.

Traditionally built. Yet peppered with solar panels, satellite dishes, and modern conveniences as carefully meshed as the hot water, Wi-Fi, and television in his room.

A muffled knock drew his eye back across the room. It took him only a moment to cross to it and open it, expecting the girl that had just left.

'I asked them to let me know when you arrived,' Georgia said, standing on the threshold of this amazing place dressed in a light, cotton-weave dress in the style of the locals, her hair peppered with tiny flowers. She breezed past him into his cave.

'Wow. Yours is much bigger than mine. Oh, you have a window.'

'You don't?'

'I have a skylight. Carved out of the top of the room. My whole room is one big arch, it's very medieval. But beautiful. And so comfortable.'

'When did you arrive?' he hedged, knowing full well because he'd taken such care not to travel with her.

'This morning. I flew in overnight and slept in the car on the way out here. You wait until you see Göreme bathed in morning light. Stunning.'

She spoke as if she'd been living here for years and he had no trouble believing it. There was something very right about the way she fitted into the natural setting. Like a local come to show him around. She set about poking around every corner of his room and checking out the balcony. 'Oh! A daybed,' she exclaimed. 'I'm thinking Casey's looked after you this trip.'

He didn't doubt it. He'd been like a bear with a sore head the past ten days so his assistant probably thought a dud room would be more than her life was worth.

'Oh, my God. Definitely the executive suite.' That came from his bathroom. He followed the sighs. She trailed her hand over every surface of a room about half the size of the open-room area again, gouged into the rock face. An enormous ornate stone bath filled the corner and he had sudden visions of slaves filling it with buckets of scented rosewater for some Turkish overlord. Or princess. Georgia peered into the void. Then turned and glared at him. 'It's a spa!' she accused.

'You're welcome to borrow it.' He laughed. Given he was only here for two nights it wasn't exactly going to see a lot of use, otherwise.

He followed her back out into the main room and onto the balcony beyond. To the front of the niche with the coffee and daybed in it was a low timber table and two old traditionally upholstered armchairs. Completely exposed to the outside air.

'Clearly Göreme doesn't get a lot of rain,' Georgia said, sinking into one of the armchairs

His lips twisted. 'Make yourself at home.'

She peered up at him and sighed. 'That's exactly what it feels like. But I've only been here a couple of hours.'

'Hospitality is obviously a traditional trade here.' Their customer service and presentation was faultless. He felt ridiculous standing over her, still dressed in his Londonwear, while she lounged there looking so comfortable and fresh and assimilated and…Turkish. 'I'm just going to change. Give me ten.'

'I'll order some drinks,' she called to his back.

The shower in that old stone bath worked as if it was brand new and it rinsed the travel grime off him no time. He pulled on a deep red T-shirt and a pair of brown shorts. As he crossed back out to Georgia he noticed he now matched the floor rug.

His own kind of assimilation.

Weeks of tension started to dissipate.

On the balcony, a different girl from the one he'd checked in with finished placing out two tall glasses of something and then she smiled at him as she ducked around the far side of the daybed niche. Yet another exit. He could well imagine spending his two days in Turkey trying to find his way out of his room. Or back to it.

Georgia leaned on the balustrade in the corner of the balcony, potted colour either side of her legs. The golden late-afternoon light blazed against her white cotton dress, making it partly translucent and thrusting a graphic reminder of the body he'd tried so hard not to ogle in the dance studio back to the forefront of his mind.

He was used to admiring Georgia's quick wit and her ready opinions and her passion for all things green. He was used to staving off the speculative zing when he brushed up against her or touched her. Or kissed her. But he was neither prepared nor sufficiently armed to manage the explosion of sexual interest that had hit him when she did that little private dance for herself in the mirror back in London. All that rippling and writhing. Nothing different from what the other women had done much more gratuitously for him but somehow so much better.

So much worse.

If she turned around right here and now and started to undulate that body he could see the shape of below her dress it wouldn't be the slightest bit out of place with the ancient curiosity of Turkey stretched out behind her. And he wouldn't be able to do a thing about standing, transfixed.

Or possibly about sweeping her up and falling down with her onto that luxury daybed just metres away.

He cleared his throat. 'Are you about to accuse me of having a better view than yours?'

She turned, smiling. 'No. The view is the same. I'm just the next level down.' She pointed down and across to a small balcony with a single chair on it. He liked the idea that he could watch her without her knowing. A small shape on the chair below caught his eye.

'You have a cat,' he said, expunging such inappropriate thoughts from his mind.

'I do. Sweet thing.'

'I think I saw its kittens at Reception.'

She smiled and it was like that breath of apple-scented air he'd taken after the long drive. 'I'm guessing there's a lot of cats in Göreme.'

He nodded. 'I'll have to get onto Casey. I seem to be missing mine.'

Her eyes glowed half with the rich light of the evening and half with a rich light all their own. 'I'll trade you cat-time for spa-time.'

He breathed her in. 'Done.'

For moments neither of them spoke, they just stood lost in each other. 'Want to go for a walk?'

No. He wanted to haul her behind him into that big, comfortable, wasted bed and not come out till morning. But that wasn't going to happen. Not outside his head. And if he was smart he wouldn't let it happen inside his head, either.

No complications.

No risk.

No Georgia.

'Sure. Show me the town.'

There was a lot to see in Göreme. They roamed all over the maze of paths and stairs and twisted byways, sometimes emerging accidentally in the private areas of people's homes and then retreating, embarrassed, despite the friendly and unsurprised response of those intruded upon. Clearly, they weren't the first tourists to end up in someone's living room. They hiked out on foot a half-hour from the town and spent the last two hours of light poring over the ancient rock-hewn world-heritage monasteries with their immaculate and stunning frescoes. A local kindly showed them back through the warren of now-dark dwellings after the sun plunged unexpectedly quickly below the horizon. Orange light glowed from almost all of them but it didn't help them a bit with their orientation.

'Thank you,' Georgia gushed as the pleased-as-punch man deposited them on the doorstep of their hotel and then waved his farewell. She wasn't totally sure Zander would find his way back to his room without assistance—she'd needed two attempts the first time for her own room—so she followed him up.

'Left,' she dropped in just at the last moment.

He turned and looked at her. 'Not right?'

'Not right.'

Left it was. One more corridor and they were at his door. 'What about dinner?' he asked.

She groaned. 'That would have been good to mention back at the entrance. We'll have to retrace our steps.'

'Hang on, I'll just get a jacket.'

He was back in moments with a light jacket over his T-shirt. Whether it was for the evening cool or whether he wasn't used to going to dinner in a T-shirt, it didn't matter. He always looked extra good in a collar so the stylish jacket was very welcome from her point of view. He'd morphed back into casual Zander as the afternoon wore on. The same man she'd spent so much time staring at and smiling at back in the King's Arms.

That was a slight analgesic against the dull ache of his rejection the past fortnight.

Discovering the city with him was a joy. His inquisitive mind and her gentle probing drew fascinating information from the locals. Twice he'd bemoaned not bringing his recorder with him on their walk to capture the lyricism and beauty of the language and the particular sound of voices as they soaked into the ancient limestone. He wouldn't make that mistake again.

The hotel had a small outdoor balcony restaurant on its roof and a serve-yourself arrangement inside. Georgia laughed at Zander's bemused expression.

'When was the last time you ate at a buffet?' she said. Though this was no ordinary buffet. Colourful fruits she'd never seen before spread out on one table and dishes of aromatic mysteries on another. She loaded a little bit of each onto a large plate and planned to round off her day of Turkish discovery here.

Some of it was odd, some of it was tasty, and two things were just plain amazing. She went back for seconds of those. They talked about the flight, the drive out, their impending early start for the balloon trip; anything they could think of that wasn't about London.

As if by agreement.

Here, they could be two totally different people. She didn't have her purposeless life or her humiliating proposal to deal with. He didn't have his work or his marathons to distract and absorb. And they didn't have the Year of Georgia between them.

Or the kiss, and what it meant.

Or his running from the dance studio. And what that meant.

She knew that she never would have achieved this amazing experience if not for the shove that Zander's radio promotion had led to. She would have drifted along in her rut for who knew how long before eventually bumping to shore and clambering out, miles off track.

'It's hard not to sit up here and feel that anything is possible,' she murmured out over the night lights of Göreme.

'Anything *is* possible.'

She laughed. 'Spoken like a true executive. For most people a lot of things are impossible. Financially, socially, time-wise.'

'You just have to get your priorities in order.' He shrugged.

She stared at him. They could make small talk or she could ask him something meaningful. 'Do you prioritise activities over personal things?'

He looked up. Cocked his head.

She sank back into her over-stuffed chair, stomach full and single drink warming her from the inside out. 'You keep yourself closed off from people, yet you're so busy and active all the time. That must be a conscious choice. It would take quite a bit of work, I would have thought, to be around people all the time but not really interact with them on a meaningful level. It must be exhausting.'

Wary eyes considered her. 'Are we talking about my staff again?'

'No. But that's a good place to start. Why do you work so hard to keep them at a distance?'

He thought about not answering. She could see it in his expression. But something tipped him the other way. 'Because I'm their manager. I don't want to be friends with them.'

'Is it that you don't know *how* to be friends with them?' Or maybe anyone.

'Pay them more and give them half-day Friday off and I'm sure they'd feel more friendly.'

'You don't buy friendship.'

'I bought yours. At fifty grand to be exact.'

That stung. Not because it wasn't true that it was his money funding her fabulous year of self-revelation, but because it cheapened what she would gladly have given him for free.

'You don't think I'd have chosen to be your friend without the Year of Georgia?'

'We never would have met without it.'

That was true. If she'd run out of his radio station a few moments earlier or later she might have been sitting here alone. Or not at all. So much of who she was finding deep inside was because of Zander's prompting. His goading.

She sat up straighter. Tired of the subterfuge. 'If we'd met in a coffee shop and I'd got to know you I would have wanted to be your friend.' Though she'd never have worked up the courage to speak to him. She'd have considered him way out of her league.

Her sub-conscious use of the past tense suddenly became remarkably apparent. Exactly when did she decide that Zander Rush was in her league?

'Is that what we are? Friends?'

'That's what I think we are. Though I know you wouldn't call it that.'

'What would I call it?'

'Acquaintance? Contact? Obligation?'

'You're not an obligation, George.'

But she *was* just an acquaintance? 'I'm sure you're not going to tell me what a great time you have trailing me all over London for my classes. Not when you bailed on the belly dancing at the first decent opportunity.'

He studied the way the dark liquid swirled in his glass. 'I owe you an explanation about that…'

'Is there even a Tuesday night network meeting?'

His eyes lifted. 'There is. That's real. But I did use it to get out of the dance class.'

She just stared.

'I wasn't…' He paused and tried again. 'I wasn't comfortable there.'

Her jaw tightened. 'Was it me or everyone else?'

He didn't answer. Her stomach sank.

*So it was her.*

'It's a very confronting form of dance when you're on the receiving end,' he said.

'You didn't look too confronted.' Until he'd looked at her. 'I was just enjoying exploring the art form.'

The intense need to justify why she'd let herself get carried away with the sensuousness of the dance washed through her.

And hot on its heels was the blazing knowledge that she owed him no apologies.

'And you should enjoy it. It's your thing,' he said.

'You're not up to spectating on a bit of sexy dancing? You didn't mind the salsa.'

'Sexy would be fine. It's just that it's…'

Colour started to show low on his jaw. Given how dim it was under the shade-sail on the hotel roof, the fact that she could see it meant it had to be a reasonable amount. Was he blushing?

'It's what?' she risked.

Embarrassing? Pathetic? Something that really shouldn't be done in public?

His eyes lifted to hers, heated. 'It's erotic.'

Her breath halted. She sagged back in her seat, dumbstruck, and crossed her hands demurely in her lap. Studying them. Then she looked out into the orange glow of the city lights far below. Then the candle of the table next to them. Taking the time to decide what to say. Taking the time to remember how to speak.

She cleared her throat and had a go. 'Erotic?'

Didn't that suggest some kind of attraction? More than just a kiss by the sea kind of attraction? More than just chemistry.

'It was very seductive.'

A sense of the same empowerment she'd felt dancing there in front of the mirror came back to her now. Dancing in front of the mirror had felt good because it was good, maybe? 'It's supposed to be seductive.'

'We don't have that kind of relationship.'

Polite Georgia burned to take the hint. To change the subject. But she was tired of being polite. Of doing what everyone expected her to. She kicked her chin up. 'You don't have that kind of relationship with the other women there, either, but you weren't running a mile from them.'

Just her.

The light came on in her mind as slow and golden as the lights of Göreme had glowed to life. But just as certain.

*Just her.*

She took a breath and whispered, 'You liked it.'

He didn't look away. But he didn't speak. He let her three words hang out there over the city, unanswered, for eternity. But finally he spoke.

'I loved it. And I shouldn't have.'

Heat to match his flared up her throat. Her gut tightened way down low. He'd loved her sensual display. 'Why?'

'Because we don't have that kind of relationship,' he repeated, his frustrated hiss more at himself than her.

She took a breath. Took a chance. 'Why don't we?'

He stared. 'What?'

'Why don't we have that relationship?'

'I'm… You're… We're doing business.'

'Why can't it be more?'

Those all-seeing eyes suddenly darted everywhere but her. 'I don't do relationships. Not of that kind.'

It was true. In the months she'd known him he never once said he couldn't do a class because he had a date. Never once mentioned anyone in his life. 'What kind do you do?'

His eyes flicked up. 'I have…encounters. Short and sharp. Over before they start.'

'One-night stands, you mean?'

'Sometimes more. But never much more.'

'Why?'

His eyes shadowed over.

'Don't you get lonely?' she breathed.

'There are worse things than being lonely.'

Like what? Being hurt? Making a wrong choice? She wondered again about what had happened to him in the past to give him that view. And what had changed in her that she was about to suggest what she was about to suggest even though she didn't feel she could ask him about his past.

'An encounter, then.' Picking up where they left off that night at Hadrian's Wall.

She'd never, ever propositioned someone so directly in her life. Even with Dan, their first time was an awkward kind of inevitable. But this didn't feel wrong. Or loose. It felt exactly as she'd felt dancing in front of that mirror.

Strong. And fated.

'Right here in Göreme. We have two nights.' Her own daring made her breathless. Was there a faster way to screw things up between them than to…well…?

'George—'

'If you're not interested, that's OK.' Knowing without a doubt that he was interested made it OK. 'But we're in a fantasy world for the next two days. We might as well get the most out of it.'

She kept her eyes on his, but it was the hardest thing she'd ever done.

'Is this a Year of Georgia thing?' he grated.

'No. This is just a Georgia thing.' She filled her lungs. 'I think we should go back downstairs.'

'What about dessert?' he asked, and it smacked of desperation.

'Do you want dessert?' she breathed, still locked onto his cautious eyes.

As she watched the caution cleared, the relief filled them, then desire. And that— finally—was what made her pulse hammer. After all the newfound confidence of the last few surreal minutes, the old doubts crept back in. Dancing in front of a mirror was one thing. Getting down and dirty—and naked— with a man like Zander was almost completely overwhelming in principle. Let alone practice.

She imagined the light cotton of her dress was the caress of sheer silk. And that helped. She imagined the respectful scarf she still wore from their explorations of the city was a face veil covering all but her eyes. She imagined the expression in Zander's gaze was the same as the one she'd caught in the mirror.

Only she didn't have to imagine that because it was. Identical. Only this one was far less repressed and infinitely more terrifying.

And exciting.

They stumbled to their feet.

'Which room?' he asked as he stood back to let her out.

Was he kidding? 'Yours. That spa is wasted on you.'

His hand burned where it pressed into her back, shepherding but also keeping a gentle contact as he urged her down the carved corridor towards the stairs. A teasing kind of torture. A perfect kind of bliss.

He bent to murmur into her ear, 'It's wasted on *just* me, maybe.'

And suddenly her mind was filled with images of the two of them tangled together in the hot opulence of the old stone bath, and her breath just about gave out. It was all she could do to keep her feet moving, but she knew if she stumbled Zander would just sweep her into his arms and carry her down the three levels to his enormous suite with its enormous bathroom and that enormous, luxurious bed.

Just like the conqueror he'd once spoken of.

He stopped at his door, turned her until the timber was at her back, and pressed into her. Peered down on her. 'Are you sure?' he murmured.

She didn't waste breath on words. Instead she pressed up onto her toes and kissed him. Showed him how sure she was. Even though this was totally out of character for her, even though she had to block thoughts of anything more future than Sunday night from her mind.

She was sure about the next two days.

This was *her* reinvention, and Zander Rush was an integral part of the new Georgia Stone. She'd never felt more certain about anything.

He hemmed her against the door with his body, his heat, and brought his hands to her face so that he could seal her acquiescence in. His tongue and his lips worked a magic just like this entire city as the cool of the earth soaked into her back.

She shivered. From delight.

'Hot bath,' he murmured, misunderstanding, and she wondered how long a big tub like the one he had inside would take to fill.

'Or hot blankets,' she whispered, but thought of the blanket of his scorching body on hers would do just fine.

He reached out with one hand, turned the doorhandle, and they fell through into the fantasy interior.

# CHAPTER NINE

THEY never made it to the bed, as it turned out. And the hot bath came quite a bit later. They got about as far as the sumptuous pillow-filled conversation niche off to the side of the room before passion got the better of them and, there, Zander made the kind of love to her that she'd never experienced before. And would never forget.

Worship.

There was no other word for it. He took the sort of care of her body—with it—that she'd only ever dreamed might happen. Measured and thorough and poignantly careful. Not tentative—she had enough aches and stretched muscles to know that he'd challenged and pushed her to be the Georgia she'd never let herself be, never needed to be, before. To roam far, far out of her comfort zone. Safe in his embrace.

She lay on her back on the daybed in the balcony niche, her head hanging back over the edge, and stared at the dark sky. Only it wasn't quite the deep black it had been when they'd first come out here, wrapped in traditionally woven blankets, wrapped in each other. It was a deep blue now, with hints of regular blue at the edges.

'Remind me to get more sleep before having sex with a marathon runner,' she murmured. Stamina? Oh, my God... 'It's nearly dawn.'

Across her legs, the heavy heat of him stirred. 'Don't we have somewhere to be at dawn?'

The balloon.

They'd come all this way to do the Cappadocian balloon experience. Could she really justify skipping it to stay here in heaven with Zander?

She sighed. Almost.

'Come on… You don't want to miss it.' He slapped her thigh gently and pushed himself into a sitting position. Dark or not, there was nothing but sky to look in on them high up on the mountain face, but within the hour the sun would be up and hot-air balloons would be rising over Göreme filled with curious, binocular-holding tourists.

And they were supposed to be in one of them.

That was the only thing that got her moving. *They.* The fact that Zander would be with her. If he wasn't booked she'd have blown the whole thing off—dream or no dream.

She padded in silence into the room with him.

What exactly did one say after a night of no-holds-barred sensual exploration?

'Let's get ready,' he said, 'and we'll get moving.'

Huh. As good as anything, she supposed.

But he tempered the banality of the words by swooping down behind her and latching onto her throat with his lips. For a bare heartbeat. Then he was gone again, gathering up his scattered clothes and rummaging in his suitcase.

She thought about running back to her room to change but, really, when you'd been awake the whole time it qualified as the same day, so slipping back into her day clothes felt acceptable.

Plenty of time to change later.

Though her eyes roamed back to Zander's big beckoning bath. She really hadn't had much chance to get clean while they were in there. Quite the opposite, in fact. She did her best to wrestle her secret, satisfied smile into submission.

It wasn't dignified to gloat.

The rush and bustle of getting out to Göreme's airfield in the still-dark of morning did a fine job of distracting her from thought, just as Zander's talented lips had done all night. Whether kissing her or murmuring conversation. It hadn't all been lascivious. They'd lain, tangled together and curled in blankets, and talked about anything that came to mind until one or other of them—or the conversation—had turned sensual again and then there was no talking for quite some time.

On arrival at the open balloon fields, four enormous bulbs glowed in the dim morning light. They lay, powerless, on their sides, and the roaring gas fires slowly filled them upright. The palest of the four lit up like its own sunrise.

'That's ours,' Zander said, coming back to her side, his digital recorder in hand.

They crossed to the enormous basket that was tethered to the ground and Georgia said a quick whisper of thanks for its size. They might look tiny in the sky but on the ground they were enormous.

She was entirely distracted and romanced by the lumbering bulbs taking shape along the roadway. Looked as if their dawn flight would be a balloon convoy. But while groups of ten and more waited for the other baskets theirs was just the two of them and their pilot.

Nice work, Casey.

'Are you my private?' A uniformed American woman stepped forward.

'EROS radio station,' Zander confirmed.

'That's you. Come on aboard and I'll give you the pre-flight information.'

By agreement, Zander recorded the whole safety presentation and the pilot put on an extra-thorough show for the media. But by the end of it Georgia certainly felt very sure about what to do if the balloon failed, and absolutely certain that it would not. The whole thing was far more regimented and controlled than she'd expected.

'I get motion-sick,' she volunteered out of nowhere and Zander looked up, surprised.

'We have bags,' the unfazed pilot said 'but you won't need them. You'll see. It's as though the planet is moving and we'll be standing still.'

Zander threaded his fingers through hers and the gentle gesture filled her with the same golden glow that kept their balloon aloft. She tightened her fingers around his as the pilot closed the door.

'Ten minutes before sun-up,' the pilot announced. 'Let's get you guys in the air.'

Zander curled Georgia into his body and stood behind her against the basket edge in the centre of the basket. She felt both sheltered and protected.

The balloon didn't rise straight up as she imagined it would when the ground crew dropped their tethers—then again her entire experience of hot-air balloons was from *The Wizard of Oz*. Instead, it skirted along, centimetres above the ground, and slowly those centimetres became meters and then Georgia got a sense of what the pilot had promised. As soon as they had some height, it suddenly felt as if the earth had started to treadmill below them and they were stationary, just hanging there in space.

The pilot gave the gas its voice and the entire balloon inhaled the burst of flame, long and steady. It rose again. Then she killed the flame and silence resumed; the only sounds were the clinking of guy ropes and the distant squeals of the passengers in the balloon ascending behind them.

Theirs breathed enormous gulps between long silent stretches and climbed and climbed in pace with the sunrise.

'Do you want to describe what you see?' Zander murmured against her neck, crossing his strong arms around her and holding the running digital recorder below her chin.

Golden light fingered out from the horizon and the deep blonde colour of the earth began to glow with a vibrancy and a gentle kind of fire. Georgia described the stunning scene, punctuated by the occasional breath of the balloon, and full of words like *God* and *heaven* and *other-worldly*. And *whole* and *healing* and *soul-breath*.

Zander and the pilot remained silent, letting her speak.

They flew over Göreme and then left it far behind as they floated over the lunar-like deserts. A distant mesa grew bigger and bigger as they approached but the pilot kept the balloon level though the others in their convoy all lifted. Georgia's adrenaline spiked and Zander's arms tightened around her, but at the last moment the pilot fired the lungs hard and their balloon soared up and over the lip of the mesa and the vast plains of Anatolia were revealed before them.

Tears filled Georgia's eyes.

Zander recorded the balloon's respiration as they drifted over great clefts in the earth and the rolling, twisting, ancient tortures of the granite and sandstone crust. He interviewed the pilot and got some close-up sounds of the clanking guy ropes and a passing flotilla of geese, generally capturing the atmosphere of this amazing experience for his listeners.

Though of course that was completely impossible to do.

This was as close to angel flight as she was going to get.

'What are you thinking about?' he murmured, back by her side and pocketing the recorder.

She spoke before she thought. 'Dying.'

He twisted around to look at her face. She laughed. 'I mean what it might be like after you die. Ascension. I'm thinking it would be like this. So…gentle and supported. No fear.'

'I didn't know you were so religious,' he murmured.

'I'm not, generally. But it's tough to be up here and not wonder…'

They fell to silence, but Zander eventually broke it.

'I remember wondering… I thought when I was young with so many people queuing up for communion there must be something in it.'

She tipped her head half back and contacted the strength of his chest. 'You're Catholic?'

'Sufficiently Catholic to have had mass at my wedding, but not to get up early every Sunday for one.'

He was close enough and smart enough to interpret the total stillness of her body—as still as the balloon felt in space—correctly.

'You're married?' she whispered.

The pilot shifted away to the far corner of the basket. If she could have climbed out to check the rigging at the crest of the balloon Georgia thought she would have.

Zander was as stiff as she was now. 'No.'

Part of her sagged with relief, but she didn't let it show. 'But you were married?'

That was a hell of a thing to be finding out now.

'Actually no.'

She turned her back on the spectacular view and looked up at him. 'But you had a wedding mass?'

His face tightened. 'We had one scheduled.'

'It didn't go ahead?' This was too important a moment to be playing word games.

'No. It was... The wedding was cancelled.'

*Oh.* 'You broke it off?'

His brows dropped. 'Why would you assume it was me?'

Because no woman in their right mind would jilt a demigod? 'I don't know. Only that you're not very pro wedding.'

Though suddenly that particular prejudice made perfect sense if he'd had a broken engagement in his past.

The gas flame belched and they rose slightly.

She tried again. 'Was it mutual?'

Zander looked out to the now blazing dawn horizon. 'No.'

Empathy washed through her. If anyone could understand the awfulness of being rejected, she could. Though she knew now that she'd never loved Dan. And Zander had clearly loved his fiancée. So how much more would that have hurt. 'I'm sorry.'

What else could she say? Better to know now than find out later? Just because she considered Dan's rejection of her proposal a dodged bullet didn't mean that was how Zander felt. And judging by the tightness of his expression and his general close-mouthedness on the subject of marriage...

Would it ever have come up if not for his slip up?

'Did she tell you why?'

'No. She and her bridesmaids fled England while the ushers were doing the friend-of-the-bride/friend-of-the-groom thing.'

Georgia's jaw dropped. 'She left you at the altar?' Didn't that only happen in movies?

He nodded. 'Even her parents weren't aware.'

*Oh, my God.* 'Zander, I don't know what to say.' Not about how awful that must have been for him. Not about the raging anger towards a woman she'd never met for hurting him so badly. Or the raging jealousy that was suddenly surging through her for some stranger he'd loved enough to marry.

'There's nothing to say.' He shrugged, but it was the least casual thing she could imagine. 'It's ancient history.'

'When was this?'

'Right out of uni.'

Fifteen years wasn't ancient. 'You were young.'

'And stupid as it turns out.'

She slid over to stand beside him so they could both look out at the beautiful, healing landscape below. 'It's not stupid to want to spend your life with someone. It's brave.'

And that was an odd word to have chosen.

He digested that for a moment. 'I wasn't brave. I think I did it because it was the right thing to do.'

'How long were you together?'

'Four years. Since final year at school. We both enrolled at Lincoln.'

*Excellent. High-school sweetheart, too.* 'You must have loved her a lot.' Maybe he still did? It would explain a lot.

He thought about that. 'I think it was one of those break-up-or-get-married moments. So I proposed.'

'And she broke up.'

'Pretty much.'

'In the worst imaginable way.'

He slid his eyes down to her. 'Strength of character wasn't one of her strong suits. She had very dominant parents.'

That wasn't a woman she could imagine him admiring. 'Hurting you was easier than facing them?'

Dark brows folded. 'Seems so.'

Cappadocia whizzed by beneath them.

'Well, I guess now I understand your cynicism about marriage. And your reaction after the promo went so wrong.'

He looked at her for the first time in minutes. 'I had to face two hundred of our family, friends, and neighbours, and tell them Lara wasn't coming. The idea that I'd set someone else up for the same public humiliation...' He shook his head.

That stole her breath every bit as much as the moment the balloon had played chicken with the sharp slope of the mesa. Her stomach lurched the same, too. In crystal-clear replay she saw the moment in the elevator all those months ago that he'd seen her distress, turned and shielded her from prying eyes with his body, and then helped her slink, unseen, from the parking garage. That was a foundation moment for her. And for him it had all been about sympathy.

'Is that what the whole Year of Georgia thing is about?' *Pity?*

'If I could have started my life over, back then, I would have. Gladly. So I was happy to be able to give you the chance.'

She stepped away, just slightly, and pretended to admire the view. But she was as taut inside as the ropes holding the two parts of their aircraft together. 'So this is your restitution?'

His voice dropped low. 'Somewhat. Making sure you got something out of it.'

Right.

Then he stepped up behind her. 'But not all of it. I can see where you're going, Georgia. Working your way to assuming I slept with you out of guilt.'

'Didn't you?'

'No. I slept with you because it was inevitable. I've been wanting to since we met.'

She slanted a look back up at him. 'It's not some twisted Year of Georgia loyalty-programme bonus class?'

His smile rivalled the sunrise. And his chuckle warmed her from the inside out. Even as she fought it. 'No. Though that suggests you learned a thing or two.'

She blew at the curl that hung over her eyes. 'You have no idea.'

He nodded slowly. She felt it against her back. 'Me, too.'

Well…this was awkward.

'So, the fifty grand was about guilt, but the sex is about… sex?'

It was stupid to hope for more. But it wouldn't be the first time her heart and her head had operated in opposition. The secret, foolish desire that she would be the one woman who he wanted more from.

His eyes shadowed over briefly. 'The fifty grand was about keeping us both out of court for breach of contract.'

And the nine hours of intensive loving…?

He lowered his voice, given the proximity of the pilot. 'Last night was about you and me and this amazing place,' he went on. 'And the attraction that's been distracting me so much for the better part of half a year.'

That sounded a lot like… 'Scratching an itch?' It sounded as awful as it felt.

He sighed heavy and hard behind her. 'Medicating a burn.'

If she needed any clue that they'd be going back to their

London lives—separately—on Monday morning, that was it. You only medicated something you wanted healed over.

Zander hadn't promised her more. She'd made her decision last night despite knowing that. So she had no grounds for complaint.

'Up ahead,' the pilot said with the best timing.

They both forced their eyes onto something other than each other and Georgia gasped as they descended amongst a field of giant, jagged pillars that stretched skywards, strong and masculine and potent.

Just like the man behind her.

'This is extraordinary,' Zander breathed, his eyes fixated on the ancient geology as their balloon bobbed amongst others over the natural wonder.

This whole weekend had been extraordinary. Living her dream just being here in Turkey, then, overnight, immersed in heaven with Zander.

But extraordinary in a bad way, too. Unravelling the origin of his anti-marriage sentiment and discovering firsthand how that was going to impact on her. No wonder he wasn't interested in risking himself again.

Zander Rush liked to take holidays from reality. But they were only mini-breaks.

First Hadrian's Wall and now Göreme. Every time they got away from London he was like a different man; he let himself indulge the attraction between them and be someone totally different from everyday Zander. Someone who communicated. Someone who laughed. Someone who loved.

Except it wasn't love. It was *medication.*

As though his connection to her was something he needed to be cured of. A temporary ailment.

Back in the real world, Zander took care to pack himself carefully away—in his big empty house, on his epic, solo marathons, in his expansive plush office. He kept everyone at arm's length. Absolutely by design.

Georgia stared out, letting the verbal spiel of the pilot wash over her: about the people of Cappadocia, about the heritage. She could hear it later on Zander's recorder. It was hard to be in this prehistoric place that had seen war and famine and death and entire civilisations come and go and worry about one man's feelings for one woman.

It seemed so trivial.

But she was that woman. This was her life. And so it wasn't trivial at all. The Year of Georgia was supposed to have taught her who she was. It was supposed to have given her a taste of what was possible and highlighted the deficiencies in her life. And it had worked.

She was Georgia Stone. For better or for worse.

Weirdly obsessed with plants, content to walk alone amongst Roman ruins, uninterested in cooking or wine appreciation or shoes, but a crack shot with a blank-pistol and the fastest code-cracker the spy school had ever seen. Terrible at the contrived sexy steps of salsa but a natural at the private undulations of belly dancing. A decent rower but a terrible swimmer. She was a lab rat and a loyal and ethical employee.

And she had a heart as protected and hidden as any of the seeds she X-rayed. But at least now she knew, without a doubt, that it was competent. That *she* was competent.

She was Georgia Stone. She would find her way.

And though she'd enjoyed the detour of the past few months, it dawned on her in realisation as blazing as Cappadocia's sun-rise that *her way* just wouldn't include Zander Rush. He'd come into her life bearing the gifts she needed to find herself again. Perhaps his cosmic role was now complete and the last twenty-four hours were just the most amazing swansong.

This conversation, this day, was her marker. He wasn't sorry about what they'd done but he wasn't interested in more and he certainly wasn't interested in for ever.

And she was.

It hit her every bit as dramatically as the Cappadocian landscape had. She wanted a for ever someone. Dan hadn't just been about keeping up with her friends. He'd been about trying to build something lasting for herself.

She wanted someone to share her life with. To explore with. To commiserate with. She was tired of being alone.

But just anyone would not do. She'd had a taste of something spectacular—someone spectacular. That was going to be very hard to go back from. And holding out for someone worthy didn't seem as scary after the six months she'd just had.

Her heart buoyed just like the envelope bobbing above their heads.

He was out there. She would find him.

But then, with the same sinking feeling that came with shutting off the gas, she accepted another hard truth.

She just wouldn't find him in this balloon.

Stalling the inevitable was easy to start with.

First, there was the business of getting the balloon back down to earth, onto the back of the pickup truck, the air out of the envelope, and the glossy fabric rolled up and stowed in the gondola. Then, there were too many ears in the bus that drove them back to Göreme to do more than smile politely at each other. Once back in the hotel, the exhaustion of twenty-four sleepless hours had claimed them both and it wasn't too hard to convince Zander that she wanted the comfort of her own room and shower for a very necessary few hours of shut-eye.

When all she wanted to do was curl up and sleep in the circle of his arms.

But now it was late afternoon and Zander stood at her door, an optimistic bottle of wine in his hand.

'Right now?' He gaped.

'My flight leaves in three hours. A car's coming for me soon.'

The wine sagged towards the stone floor. 'Why?'

'Emergency at work,' she lied.

He lifted one brow. 'A seed emergency?'

Defensiveness made her rash. 'I don't remember signing anything that gave you say over what I do with my private time.'

He didn't bite, though he did glance around him in the dim hallway. 'May I come in?'

'I'm packing.' Truth was she was already packed because, even though she desperately needed it, sleep had evaded her. But her suitcase lay conveniently open on her luxurious, plump bed. She stood back so he could enter.

'What's going on, Georgia?'

'Nothing. I just have to get back.'

'Your seed emergency. Right.' He placed the wine on the table. 'What's really going on?'

He had to know. Surely.

She shrugged. 'We've done Göreme. We've done the ballooning. We're done.' In more ways than one.

'But you were so keen to see Cappadocia.'

'And I'm already planning on coming back for a longer stay.'

'This is about last night.' It wasn't a question.

'Last night was…' What did more cosmopolitan people say at this moment. Fun? Wild? Memorable? 'Last night was a one-off.'

The eyebrow quirked again. 'Really? And you felt the need to fly out of the country to avoid a repeat?'

'I didn't want to hurt your feelings.'

He snorted. 'Right. This is much easier on my feelings.'

His sarcasm triggered hers. 'I'm not really up on the protocols of dis-entanglement.'

He repeated the word, silently. 'Wow.'

'Zander—'

'For someone inexperienced in the art of casual sex you certainly are a quick study at the kiss-off part.'

'This isn't a—'

'Yeah, Georgia, it is. But what makes you so sure I was even offering a round two?'

'I...' That took the wind from her sails. 'You turned up with wine.'

He held the bottle up. The text was in Turkish but the image on the label was of a big balloon flying over Cappadocia. 'It was a keepsake. I got me one, too.'

*Oh.*

'If I hadn't knocked would you have even told me you were leaving?'

'Of course!' But not until the very last minute. And he seemed to know it.

'You don't have to leave, Georgia. If last night was a mistake for you, then fine. We can keep our distance until tomorrow. But this is your trip. You've wanted this for ages.'

'I can't—' *Be here. With you. And not be with you.* 'It's time to go.'

'You don't trust me.' Again, not a question.

'Of course I do.' She sighed. She didn't know anyone she trusted more. Dan included.

'So what's the problem?' Awareness blinked to light in his grey eyes. 'Unless you don't trust yourself.'

She just stared.

'That's it, isn't it? If you stay you don't trust yourself to stick to your own resolution.' Triumph glossed over his anger. He stepped closer. 'So if you want me,' he went on, 'why are you leaving?'

'I don't want you.' *I don't want to want you.*

'Liar.'

Yeah, she was. 'This was an aberration, remember?'

He frowned. Clearly he didn't remember saying it.

'Besides today, tomorrow, what does it matter when we finish it?' she asked. 'Or do you just like to control the use-by dates on your affairs?'

Lord. That word sounded both very grown up and very old-fashioned at the same time.

His lips thinned. 'I just want to understand it, Georgia. To understand you.'

Something made her ask. 'It would have finished tomorrow, wouldn't it, Zander?'

He tensed up.

'Because this isn't real. You said it yourself, you and me in this fantasy place. We would have ended the moment we touched down in London.' He didn't contradict her. 'So what's a few hours between friends?'

His eyes narrowed. 'Friends?'

'Unless I've misunderstood you,' she risked. 'If you wanted something more long-term, Zander, now's your chance. Just say.' Because she'd be up for it.

His lips pressed tighter together. His eyes roiled.

She held on longer than was good for her dignity, just in case. But still he stood silent. As expected.

'So, now that we're on the same page,' she said, heartsore, 'I'm exercising my right to choose. And I choose out.'

She sounded much calmer than she felt.

'I guess I should thank you,' he said after a long, silent age.

'What for?' Giving herself so wholeheartedly to him?

'At least this time I won't have to explain myself to two hundred people.'

Her heart sank. She hadn't even considered the similarities to his runaway bride. But the two situations were nothing alike. Were they?

'I'm not running out on you.' Yeah, she was. Avoiding the whole situation. 'I'll see you in London.'

'Business as usual.'

'Is there another way?'

She longed for him to say there was. She longed for him to say, *Stay and we can be a couple.* She longed for him to tell her she meant enough to him to break his work-only rules for.

But he wouldn't.

And they both knew it.

He scooped the wine up and placed it carefully in the centre of her open suitcase protected by her intimates. Then he turned back to her and spoke.

'See you in London.'

And then he was gone.

# CHAPTER TEN

*November*

*THWACK.*

Her arrow hit the target, not quite as close as she was aiming but at least it found purchase. She lowered the bow.

Indoor archery—the latest on her list. Actually, it was supposed to be outdoor archery but it was the dying days of November and autumn had already dragged as interminably as her mood. The Year of Georgia was galloping by and would be over before there was any further warm weather, so indoors it was.

She and Zander were back to the early days of her Year of Georgia classes—politely civil. He came to exactly as few classes as he needed to get the monthly segments done and he seemed to have lost his enthusiasm for recording everything—much more sound than he needed. But the segments were proving unexpectedly popular with EROS' listeners and so he had to keep producing them, even when she thought he would probably have preferred to just let the whole thing go. Maybe buy out her contract personally to be rid of the hassle.

They'd had their promotional value well and truly. Twice over. Every time a segment aired people remembered Dan, too, and there was a flurry of general media attention about where he was. What he was doing.

Who he was doing.

He'd been seen around town with someone. A woman. The same woman. So at least one of them had managed to find their way out of the mire to a regular sort of relationship. Although as fast as the gossip had come that they were on, it seemed as if maybe they were off again.

For her part, she surprised herself by discovering that even being given everything money could buy got old. She was tired of the Year of Georgia. She was tired of smiling politely at Zander and speaking into his digital recorder and pretending everything was fine.

Everything was not fine.

He filled her consciousness when he was around and plagued her thoughts when he wasn't. She sat in life-drawing class looking at a phenomenally proportioned naked male model and all she could think about was Zander's proportions. The curve of his strong shoulder. The gentle undulation of his throat. If her drawings never looked like the man she was sketching it was because they generally looked more like Zander.

Having asked Casey to strip her schedule of anything resembling Egyptian stone therapy and deep muscle massage, she begged Zander's assistant to put them back in. If only to relieve the new tension she lived with these days.

They helped, but only for an hour or so each week. Then the lingering dissatisfaction and un-rightness returned and troubled her until the following week.

Float tanks, hypnosis, Bowen therapy—she tried something new every week for months. And nothing helped quite like the moment Zander walked into her class. The precious seconds before her brain reminded her not to get so excited. For those few breaths all the tension drained from her body.

She lived for those moments.

His garden was progressing, he'd told her one week, before passing her his phone to have a look at the design that flourished under the care of his landscaper. Irrational, blazing envy tormented her that she didn't get to prune it or mow it or love it herself.

But she just smiled and said, 'That's great,' and handed the phone back.

Another week he played her the completed Cappadocia segment and her heart squeezed both for the memories of Turkey and for the sublimely neutral expression on his face. Totally untroubled.

She equally envied and grew infuriated by his lack of concern.

Turning it off like that was a gift. Just not a very nice one.

'Nice shot,' Zander murmured, off to one side as a helper ran in and pried her arrow from the target.

*Nice condescension*, she thought. But aloud she only thanked him. She lined up another arrow. The Amazons must have had some serious upper-body muscles because doing this just once a week had given her a perpetual muscle ache in her chest.

Unless that was just her heart.

'To the left,' he murmured from her right side. She ignored him. 'Your left, not my left.'

She lowered her bow and turned. 'Seriously, Zander? You're going to back-seat drive?'

'Here...'

He stepped in behind her and told her to assume the firing position. Then he slid one hand along her extended bow arm and curled the other around her pulled back firing arm. And he reoriented her the tiniest bit to the left.

'Just a smidge.'

'Is that a professional archery measure?' she muttered through tight teeth.

His laugh was a puff of warm air against her ear and her whole neck broke out in gooseflesh.

'Yes, it is.'

'You know this because of your many years of competition in the sport.' At the very last second she realised he *could* have archery experience. It was a solo enough sport to be right up his alley.

'I miss you,' he said, as though that was exactly what they'd just been talking about. And maybe they had.

'You miss the sex.'

'No. I could get that anywhere.' *Charming*. 'I miss you. I miss your conversation and your snark. I just wanted to feel you. Just for a moment.'

She stood stiff and unyielding in his arms. It was the hardest thing she'd ever had to do. Even her eyes didn't waver from the target across the room. 'And have you had your fill of feeling me up?'

'George—'

The way he said her name…it caused her bow arm to tremble. She forced it to stillness.

'—do you have to drag it down to such a level?'

'What level should it be at? You're not interested in a relationship but you're not above a bit of casual sport at my expense?'

His arms dropped. Not scorched, but definitely not relaxed. 'I hate this.'

'Not my fault. You set the rules.'

'I don't recall making any rules.'

'By implication.' She lowered her bow. There was no way it was safe to fire an arrow while she was this distracted. But she didn't turn around. 'Or have you changed your mind about relationships?'

'Why can't we just…feel our way?'

She turned. 'Are you asking me on a date?'

Instantly he stiffened. 'I'm… No. Aren't we a bit beyond dates?'

'So you're asking me just to sleep with you at your request?'

His brow folded. 'No. George—'

'You're offering me sex with no commitment, Zander,' she pointed out. 'And that can't work.'

And, astonishingly, she saw clearly for the first time why. But he couldn't. 'Why not?'

An insane kind of lightness flooded her. 'Because I know who I am, now. And I know why I proposed to Dan.' Even though it had been unconscious. To bring his lack of commitment to a head. And sure enough the very next relationship she walked into was the same. Worse.

'What's Dan got to do with this?'

'Nothing. And everything. Dan had a dozen little ways of keeping me at emotional arm's length. You have a hundred.'

He lowered his head.

'I don't want to beg and scrounge for scraps of emotional intimacy,' she said. 'I'm worth more than that.'

'No one's going to promise you a ring before you even begin exploring who you are as a couple, George.'

His words cut deep. But she stayed strong. 'You've ruled a commitment out right from the start. Why would I set myself up for that?'

'Because of what we have?'

'What do we have? Cracking chemistry? Intellectual compatibility?' She started packing up her gear. 'You're either condemning me to still be waiting for you to throw me a bone when I'm eighty or a courteous breakup in two years when you tire of me. Either way I lose.'

'You're losing now.'

It wasn't conceit. She absolutely *was* losing. 'I'm cutting my losses.'

'So that's it? New improved Georgia wants all or nothing?'

'No.' She looked up at him. 'I definitely want it all. But I'll choose nothing if I have to.'

He stared, thinking. 'Maybe I'll change my mind?'

'Really, Zander? Based on what? Give me some criteria for what will mean you can get over what happened to you in the past.'

His lips thinned.

'Because otherwise you're expecting me to just limp along hoping I'm being the kind of girlfriend that a man like you changes his mind for. That I'm saying the right things, doing the right things, wearing the right things. Dying a thousand deaths every time I find that maybe I'm not.'

'George—'

'I'm not negotiating, Zander, I'm explaining. I'm telling you why I'm choosing nothing, because everything is not on the cards with you.'

He hissed his displeasure.

She took a long breath. 'I'll come back for the Valentine's show but you should have enough audio to carry you through Christmas and January. I'm done rediscovering myself. I'm done with classes.'

'You still have twenty thousand left—'

'You can keep the change.'

In more ways than one.

'Wait…' But he had nothing to say after that.

She took a breath. Took a chance. Exhausted from holding it in. And lying to herself. 'I love you, Zander. I love your dedication to your sport, I love your hermit ways, I love your big, pointless garden, and the joy I saw on your face in Turkey. I want it all with you. What are you going to do about it?'

His eyes flared. He stared.

But said nothing.

Her heart crumpled inwards as if it were vacuum sealed. 'And there we go.'

She picked up her bag and moved to the door. He stopped her with a hand on her arm. Gentle. Uncertain.

'So that's it? I'm not going to see you again?'

'Isn't that how you prefer your life? As empty as your house? Surely it must be easier to keep yourself from forming relationships that way.' She curled her fingers around his. 'This isn't judgement, Zander. This is my choice.'

He stared, then dropped his eyes to her fingers as she used them to unclasp his from her arm.

'Goodbye, Zander. Good luck.'

And then she walked out. Straight. Steady.

Just as an arrow through the heart should be.

# CHAPTER ELEVEN

*February*

THERE was only so much thermal a man could wear and still run comfortably. February meant he moved most of his outdoor exploits indoors. He hit the treadmill instead of the highways, and he did endless laps of his grand staircase and reacquainted himself with his friendly neighbourhood indoor-climbing facility in lieu of hiking.

It kept his event fitness up and his time occupied. In body if not in spirit.

'Mr Rush,' the guy belaying his stack said. He'd been coming here every winter for the last six years but still he was Mr Rush to them all. He'd never invited them to call him anything else.

*It's Zander…*he imagined saying.

How hard could that be to say? Just a few short syllables. But the words were an overture for something else, something he wasn't in a hurry to have. Acquaintances. God forbid, *friends*. You told a guy your Christian name one week and you were helping him move house the next.

Georgia had accused him of having a hundred ways of keeping her at an emotional distance. Maybe that kind of thinking was just one of them. Most people would be too polite to push past that kind of passive resistance. And only some people had what it took to sneak past it.

Georgia had it. Straight in under his skin. Between his ribs. Into his thoracic cavity where his heart hung out.

He'd never imagined that having all his time back just for himself would be such a burden. He'd whinged long and hard to Casey about Georgia's endless classes, the impost on his time, and she'd tutted and said all the things a boss liked to hear—*Yes, Mr Rush. I'll see to it, Mr Rush*—yet, somehow they'd snuck up on him and started to feel normal. So that when they were gone he felt…

Bereft.

As if a part of him were missing. Yet it was much bigger than the sum total of the hours he'd put in at class.

He smiled at his spotter as he finished fixing his rigging. 'Thanks, Roger.'

See…Roger. How hard was that? But still he didn't say it. *Call me Zander.*

He forced his mind off his bloody social skills and onto the stack ahead of him. Newcomers climbed the left—hard but civilised—regulars got the fierce alignment. A good brutal climb was definitely in order.

It worked for about six minutes. People thought the point of indoor climbing was to spider monkey up the fastest, like some kind of country-fair attraction. For a free stuffed elephant. To him, the point of indoor climbing was stamina and endurance. Taking it slow and making it hard. Making it hurt.

Pain had a way of putting everything else into perspective.

Except today. Today it wasn't working.

*Isn't that how you prefer your life?* she'd said. *As empty as your house?*

No, actually it wasn't. He liked it quiet. He liked it predictable and undemanding. But he didn't actually choose empty. Empty chose him. When you worked as hard and as long as he did, when you had the kind of responsibility the network had entrusted him with and the kind of income they offered, then there really wasn't a lot of room for anything *but* empty.

Of course Georgia would have called those excuses. She would have asked him what he really wanted to do with his life and then challenged him to do it. No matter what.

Which kind of relied on him knowing what he wanted to do. And he had no idea.

He just knew what he was doing now definitely wasn't it.

His hand slipped on a misplaced transfer and he slammed hard against the wall, braced only on one foot peg, two fingers taking his entire weight.

Now wasn't it. The network wasn't it. EROS wasn't it.

The enormous gulf those missing classes had left started to make some sense. He'd enjoyed those. A lot. Recording the experiences, capturing people's stories. He'd exercised creative muscles that he'd let wither over the past corporate decade. He'd plucked remembered strands from something he'd been passionate about before the network. Before Lara.

His roots.

And audio production was a thousand miles from what he was doing now. What he'd grown rich and famous on.

What he'd grown empty on.

He tried not to imagine his big empty house, because every time he did the same thing happened. He saw it full of life, and colour.

And Georgia.

She'd planted the seeds of herself as surely in his imagination as she did plants in her garden. And she'd grown there, like some kind of invasive creeper vine. Tangling. Binding.

Bonding.

Until he could barely separate the reality of what he was left with from the fantasy of his imagination.

'Bloody hell.'

A grunt to his left drew him out of his self-obsessed focus. How long had he been hanging here, not moving? Roger knew him too well to think he was in difficulty, but while he was off absorbed in fanciful thoughts another climber had managed to get fully rigged and halfway up the wall. Albeit the easier configuration.

He turned to look at the new guy and nearly lost his finger hold again.

Bradford.

No question. He'd been in enough newspaper articles and on enough gossip sites to be recognisable anywhere. Even sweaty and bulging on a rockface. However simulated.

An insane rage overcame him.

This man had rejected Georgia. She gifted him her unique heart—she risked and exposed herself—and this guy thought himself too good for her. He hadn't fought for her when she ended it and he'd wasted no time in picking up with someone new once he was free to.

Bradford glanced at him, frowning, and then very purposefully climbed ahead.

Every hormone in Zander's body urged him to speak. To demand Bradford justify himself. Explain in what universe hurting the most gentle, courageous woman on the planet was acceptable. Except then he remembered that he'd done effectively the same thing and much more recently.

Rejected her.

Returned the gift of her love. Unopened.

Let her go without a fight.

And he realised that Bradford was no more suited to for ever with a woman like Georgia than he was. And no more worthy.

He signalled Roger, below, leaned back, and zipped to the floor. He fumbled his way out of the climbing gear in his haste and left it where it lay.

And he got the hell out of there before he asked Bradford the only thing he really wanted to know.

*How did you get over her?*

* * *

A year.

An entire year had gone past since she'd last sat in EROS' broadcast studios. Actually, it wasn't the same studio, it was a twin, the mirror image of the one through the tinted glass that she'd first sprinted from twelve months ago when Dan turned her proposal down.

Back then she'd thought that nothing could be worse than standing in the elevator with the aghast curiosity of the station's entire staff directed at her, begging the doors to close.

But coming back in here, today, was infinitely worse.

Back into Zander's territory.

The man she hadn't seen for over two months. A man she'd longed for over Christmas and cried for at New Year and absolutely dreaded seeing as Valentine's Day approached.

A day of love and celebration.

Ugh.

'Can I offer you a coffee?' the segment producer said.

Yes. A warm drink would take the February chill from her fingers even if it couldn't do anything for the one in her heart. She knew because she'd been trying these past months. 'Tea, please?'

The producer shot a look at the teenaged girl by her side and she scarpered off to make Georgia's tea, flushing.

'Work experience,' the producer grunted, tossing her hair.

*Dogsbody*, Georgia thought and instantly sided with the kid.

'Have a seat,' the woman said, and then, as Georgia sat, she added, 'So you were sent the questions?'

'Yes.' And she had notes for her answers. 'What was the best activity? What will I be keeping up after today? What did I learn from my year?'

'If there's anything off-script you'd like to add, you can go for it.'

Anything about Dan, she meant. The station was as good as their word—he'd not been mentioned since she first signed the contract.

'If it comes up,' she agreed. But nothing more. She wasn't going to be pressured on her last moments under EROS' power.

'I've heard Zander's final segment,' the producer said. 'It's good.'

Georgia tried not to stiffen at the mere mention of his name.

'Speak of the devil…' one of the announcers murmured without the slightest change in facial expression and she did stiffen, then. Fully. But turning to look would have been too obvious.

The producer also pretended not to notice his arrival in the studio next to theirs, but her eyes flicked briefly to the darkened glass behind Georgia. 'Great. Nothing like being watched to improve performance,' she muttered while slightly diverting her face.

The announcer laughed.

The disrespect at Zander's expense irked Georgia. She might have cut all ties with him but this was their boss they were sniggering about. A decent—if complicated—man, with a tough job to do.

'Don't worry,' the producer said, misreading her face and leaning in to pretend to adjust Georgia's headset. 'He can't hear us until I press the button. Soundproof.'

'Then you'd better hope he can't lip-read,' she murmured.

Defending him was strangely pleasurable. Was she that desperate for a connection between them? Walking in here today was fifty per cent pain and fifty per cent anticipation that she might find him standing in the hallway.

Where she'd first seen him.

But no, he'd been predictably absent.

Until now.

'Guess he's more interested than usual because they're his segments.' The producer tried to cover her gaffe.

Or he just wanted to see her without being seen.

Hopeless optimist.

'Have I got time to go to the Ladies'?' Georgia asked, out of nowhere, then tried to add veracity to her lie. 'Nervous pee.'

The producer huffed. They'd just got her settled and all wired up. 'If you're quick.'

She scooted up out of her seat and crossed to the door without paying the tinted glass the slightest attention. Outside she turned right and walked in the opposite direction to the staff toilets.

She opened the next door without knocking.

'Zander...'

He spun by the tinted glass in the half shadows. The studio on the other side was fully lit and much easier to see than he had been in reverse. She did her best to stay back in the shadows, out of view of gossipy eyes.

'Georgia.' He swallowed. 'How are you?'

'I'm good. And you?'

'Good.'

Excellent. That meant they were both crap. 'I wanted to ask you about the cheque.'

'That money is yours. You shouldn't be penalised for your thrift.'

Thrift. That made her sound about as exciting as a dusty old book. 'Twenty thousand pounds, though?'

He shrugged. 'You earned it. What will you do with it?'

She hadn't let herself think. 'Maybe back to Turkey?'

'You should. See it properly.'

'There's so many options once you have actual money in your hands,' she breathed.

'You can do whatever you want. I hope you enjoy it.'

His sincerity struck her. And why not? She wouldn't have fallen in love with a man who wasn't genuinely lovely.

'Why are you hiding in here?' she asked.

'I'm not hiding, I'm monitoring.'

'That seems to have upset your staff.'

He smiled, not the slightest bit sorry. 'I'm sure. Some of them are big on fame and short on accountability.'

Silence fell. Next door the work-experience girl reappeared with her cuppa and glanced around anxiously.

Georgia pushed away from the wall. 'Well, I should go.'

'Are you nervous?' he asked.

Yes, and not just because she was going on air. 'A bit. This is going to be hard for me.'

'I've been very clear on the limitations. Anyone who mentions Bradford will be collecting unemployment next week.'

The kindness touched her. And his total obliviousness hurt her lungs. 'Thank you.'

'I heard about his new girlfriend,' Zander risked. 'How do you feel about that?'

Feel? 'I'm happy for him.'

'I worried for you. That you might—'

'Take it personally?'

He dropped his eyes.

'I'm not going to say I loved the implication of him finding someone so soon. That it must have been me that made the two of us a bad fit.'

'That's not how it works.'

'Yeah, it does. Finding someone you can spend your life with is rare enough so the chances of both people finding that someone in each other...' She left the rest unsaid. 'Truly,' she reassured. 'He seems really content. It's been a tough year for him but he's found his reward.'

Zander stared. Breathed out slowly. 'You're a good person, Georgia Stone.'

She lifted her chin. 'I know. I'd be my friend if I wasn't already me.'

His lips parted in a classic Zander chuckle.

'I'd better go. Your producer's taking my absence out on your work-experience girl.'

He looked into the bright booth and she turned for the

door. His voice stopped her just as she reached for the handle. 'Georgia...'

She turned.

'You're looking good.'

No, she looked pretty much the same as she always did. With the exception of the grey smudges under her eyes that she'd worked hard to disguise. 'Thank you.'

'And you're sounding good.'

She could easily have said something flippant, but these might be the last words they ever exchanged. She wanted them to count. 'I am good. I'm finally doing what makes me happy. Regardless of what everyone else expects. It's very...healthy.'

'Healthy.' He turned the word over on his lips. 'It's very compelling.'

Her chest tightened. Two minutes before going live on air was not the time to mess with a woman's head. 'See you later, Zander.'

Though, no, she wouldn't. Not after today.

Today was the end.

She stepped back out into the full fluoro-brightness of the radio station and crossed back to her own studio. She smiled at the young girl who passed her a cup of tea as she walked in and let the producer set her up with her headphones and mic, again. And she did a cracking job of ignoring Zander's presence. Even though she could barely see him now in the darkened studio next door, she felt his every breath.

The two announcers ran through a barrage of vocal warm-ups, which she figured were mostly for show, and she gave the young girl now inside the control box two thumbs up for a great cuppa.

Amazingly the hot drink did help, just slightly.

'Thirty seconds,' the producer announced over the studio loudspeaker, and the sudden sound of commercials filled the room. The announcers sat, smiled at her, and readied themselves.

Georgia took a deep breath and forced her mind off the man whose gaze burned into her back.

'You're listening to EROS: all the best music all the time. We're back with The Valentine Girl, Georgia Stone, who has just finished the most amazing year of self-discovery. Georgia—' the announcer was gifted at sounding as if he hadn't used the last song break to go over in detail what they were about to say '—what was the highlight of your year?'

She leaned a little more into the microphone and did her best to imagine she was speaking only to her gran, not to three million Londoners. 'There was a moment, just a heartbeat really, high above Cappadocia in the balloon, when everything in my life just—' she struggled for the right word, then found it '—reconciled.'

'Reconciled?' the younger announcer said.

'Everything just clicked. Into place. And I knew that I'd found what I was looking for.'

'What were you looking for?'

She forced herself not to even flinch in Zander's direction. 'Myself, mostly.'

'That sounds very Zen.' The second announcer giggled, dubiously.

*Introspection.* Broadcasting death, Zander had warned her all those months ago. She closed her eyes and gave in. 'And spy school was pretty cool, too.'

And they were off…asking with enormous relief how she'd felt firing a gun and what it was about numerical codes that made her such a natural at solving them.

*Empowered* and *no idea* were the respective answers.

'An empowered woman with a gun in her hands, look out!' the male announcer said.

Georgia didn't even bother laughing out of courtesy.

The man's eyes flicked up to the control booth window where the producer was making uninterpretable hand signals.

'We're going to take some of your calls now...' the announcer said. He glanced at his computer monitor. 'Lucinda from Epping, go ahead.'

Lucinda from Epping wanted to wax lyrical about belly dancing and how much she enjoyed it since starting it on Georgia's recommendation. She was easy to enthuse with because the belly dancing was something she'd kept up even after the necessity to go had ended. It was somewhere she could escape back to Göreme in her mind. Back to Zander.

And back to the way he'd made her feel when his arms were around her.

Russell from Orpington wanted to complain about his girl-friend and her high standards and how impossible it was for an ordinary man to meet the expectations of empowered women.

'Just try, Russell,' she murmured. 'None of us are looking for perfection. Just a decent effort.'

That even birthed a knowing smirk between the surly producer and her teenaged slave.

'Alex from Hampstead. You've had your own—' the young announcer stared at his computer screen and did his best to pronounce what was obviously an unfamiliar word '—epiphany?'

'That's Alek,' the quiet voice said, and Georgia tightened up like a barrel bolt. 'With a *K*.'

The announcer rolled his eyes. 'Clock's ticking, mate.'

Could they not hear it? She glanced between them all and none of them seemed to have the vaguest idea that it was their boss on the line. Her chest started to rise and fall. She forced herself not to turn around but her inner eye was focused squarely on the glass of the mirrored studio behind her.

'I've had exactly the same moment,' Zander murmured down the line. 'That moment where everything just falls into place and works. Effortless.'

'It's a great feeling,' Georgia pressed past her dry throat. Was he talking about his engagement fifteen years ago?

'And once you've had it and then you lose it it's…intolerable. Worse than never having it at all.'

Yeah, he was. Her chest tightened up.

'But once you've had it,' she whispered, 'then you at least know what to strive for. You know what your bar is.'

'True.'

And she didn't meet his bar the way every man out there would struggle to meet Zander's.

The announcer glanced at his producer for assistance; clearly this wasn't his idea of riveting radio.

'What if you fear you'll never reach it again?' Zander said, low and personal.

His voice, in her earphones, was like lying on that daybed in Göreme with him. Intimate. Breathless. She closed her eyes, pressed the ear pads harder to her head to keep him close. To keep it private.

'If you reached it once,' she whispered, 'then you know you *can* reach it again.'

Even though he was talking about his fiancée, she hated the pain she heard in his voice. She loved him; she didn't want him suffering. The way she was.

'Is that what you believe?' he murmured.

'I have to. Or I'd go crazy wondering if I let the best thing in my world go.'

The announcer suddenly saw an in. 'And someone else has snapped him up now,' he said.

Georgia's eyes flew open and her stomach heaved. Had Zander moved on already? 'What?'

'Your ex. He's spoken for.'

Relief and anger pulsed under her skin in equal measures. Daniel. Not Zander.

The producer's lips formed a string of swearwords clear enough to be readable even by her. The announcer seemed to remember he wasn't supposed to mention Dan. He flushed to his roots. And then paled.

She wondered if Zander hadn't exaggerated how stern a warning he'd given them all.

Silence screamed live on air. She was so conscious that she had to say something. 'I still adore Dan.' She picked her way carefully to an answer. 'But, no, I wasn't talking about him.'

'Aren't you going to ask me where it was?' Zander murmured down the line.

The announcer circled his finger above his head, signalling his producer to wind up the call. She moved to disconnect the call.

'No!' Georgia said out loud and stilled the announcer's gyrofinger and the producer's steps.

'No?' The husky voice grew amused.

'Not you, *Alek*,' she corrected, matching the warmth. 'So go ahead. Where did you have this epiphany?'

How could she be alone in the dark with Zander when three million people were listening? Yet she just didn't care.

'There's a tiny town up near the Scottish border. Great for viewing sunsets.'

Her breath caught.

The radio staff threw up their hands in silent protest as their segment started to unravel before their eyes.

'I kissed a woman there and it changed my life.'

The blood rushed from her face. 'A kiss can't change your life. Only you can do that.'

'I'm beginning to understand that.'

Both announcers and the producer all snapped their focus behind her and their mouths gaped open. She turned and saw the studio lights now fully blazing next door. Illuminating Zander leaning casually up against the glass, his mobile phone to his ear.

'You taught me that,' he said.

Georgia stared, lost in the fixed focus of his eyes. 'I did?'

'I watched you week after week, plunging into situations that you weren't comfortable with, taking the best parts out of them. Always positive. Always interested in the people you met. You only had to do the minimum but you didn't, you applied yourself fully to it.'

'I wanted to fix myself.'

'You weren't broken. You never were. You're perfect the way you are.'

'Perfectly crazy?' She smiled through her tears.

'Perfectly competent.' He tipped his head. 'I want to be competent, too.'

'You are.'

'No. I'm not. I do a job I hate because someone once told me I was good at it. I live a life I hate because someone once convinced me I wasn't worthy of better.'

Lara.

She stood and tugged her headphones and mic with her. They were her lifeline. An umbilical cord to Zander. She crossed to the glass. '*She* was never worthy of *you*.'

'I believe that now. It's taken a long time. She didn't have your courage. Your character.'

No, she didn't. 'What life would you lead, if you could choose?' This moment was too important to care whether EROS' listeners were interested. They might have gone to a commercial for all she knew.

'I want to go back to my roots. Making audio documentaries for syndication. It's what I always wanted to do.'

She thought about all those unnecessary hours of additional sound he'd recorded. 'Is there a market for that?'

'I'll make a market. My house would make a great studio.'

She smiled. His optimism was so infectious.

She placed her small hand on the glass, over his large one where he leaned on it. His eyes glowed down into hers. 'What else?' she whispered.

'I'm going to travel more. See amazing things. Record amazing things. My world has grown way too tiny.'

'You won't be able to travel.' She laughed, though it was more of a cry. 'You'll be poor.'

'You forget, I run marathons. I'll run the world on foot if I have to.'

He would, too, this new Zander. The best of the two Zanders. A tear streaked down her face. She curled her fingers on the glass and wished she could touch his.

'What else?'

'I'm going to get a new gardener.'

The rapid change in direction threw her. 'What happened to Tony?'

He shrugged and smiled, but it was nervous. 'Tony won't live in.'

'You want a live-in gardener?' He might not be able to afford that, either.

He nodded. 'If you're free.'

Behind her, the announcers gasped, as one. And it saved her the trouble.

She had to swallow twice to get the words out. 'You want me to be your gardener?'

He curled his fingers to match hers. 'I want you to have the garden. And you're going to need to tend to it every day.'

'You want me to live in your house?' she whispered.

'For ever, George. With me.'

'But you don't want to get married? You told me.'

He shook his head. 'I didn't want to get hurt. But that hasn't worked. I hurt every day because I'm not with you. So I'm cutting my losses.'

All over London women probably gasped, but Georgia knew exactly what that meant.

*'Ever the romantic, Alek,'* an announcer said in both their ears.

Zander didn't laugh. Neither did she.

'I love you, Georgia,' he whispered through the glass, down the line and out of three million radio speakers. 'I thought I was managing the rest of my life but the moments with you were like a blazing beacon and they spilled light on just how dull the rest of my existence has become.' He took a breath. 'It's lucrative but it's nothing without you. Totally empty.'

Tears clogged her throat. She struggled to clear them.

*'Are you proposing, Alek?'* the second announcer prompted, scenting a ratings slaughter.

'Marriage? No,' he breathed, and her heart lurched. 'When I do that I'll do it somewhere infinitely more special than my workplace.' He tucked his phone to his ear and pressed a second hand up against the glass. 'But I am proposing a future. A life together. A second chance for both of us.'

Georgia stared at him through the glass, speechless. Then she ripped her headphones and mic off and turned for the door.

The announcers went into panic mode but she didn't care. They'd talk their way out of it; they always did. They could earn their enormous pay. She threw her gratitude to the young work-experience girl, grinning from ear to ear, who held the studio door open for her so that she could practically run through it.

Outside, the whole office stood, transfixed, staring at the studio doors. She ignored them. Except for Casey who bounced on two feet, tears streaming down her face, both hands pressed to her excited mouth.

Zander met her the moment she burst through the door. Swept her up and locked her to his strong body, turning slowly, eyes squeezed shut.

'I'm so sorry,' he murmured over and over.

'For what?' she gasped, lifting her face from the crook of his neck. 'Practically proposing on air?'

'For letting you go. For making you go.'

'I needed to stand alone. I needed to find that part of myself and know I could survive it.'

He sighed. 'Your courage shamed me.'

'No…'

'But it inspired me, too. To be authentic. To risk everything.'

'Did you think I'd say no?'

'I wasn't thinking. I wasn't planning on calling in when I went into that studio. I just saw you and you were so radiant and...*fine*...it boiled my blood.'

She tipped her head. 'It made you angry that I was doing well?'

'It made me angry that I wasn't. I *so* wasn't. And I realised why the moment you walked back out of this studio. You took all the light with you.'

'And you want me to live in your house?'

'I want us to be together. I think I've been sitting in that house just waiting for it to populate itself with a family. A family I didn't want. But, truthfully, I don't care where we live. In fact, I'd be really happy to go back to Göreme and grow old underground with you. Whatever you want.'

Heat filled her cheeks. 'I really want your garden.'

His lips turned up slightly at the corners. 'Just the garden?'

'No,' she breathed. 'I really want you.'

She lifted her lips and Zander pulled her up closer in his arms to help close the distance. They clung together, sealing their promise in flesh.

On the other side of the glass the two announcers were exploding with mute action, like a pair of mime race-callers. Georgia feared for exactly what was being said but, after the year they'd had, really, how bad could it be?

'I'm sorry we're not going to be rich,' he whispered against her lips.

'I don't want to be rich.'

'I wanted to give you the world.'

She traced his jawline with her finger. 'You already have. Besides,' she said, breathless, 'I'm only cash-poor.'

He frowned. 'But your flat...'

'It's one of four in the complex,' she reminded him. And he nodded. So she broke the news. 'I own them all.'

He just gaped.

'Well, technically the bank owns them all but, you said yourself, I'm thrifty. When all my friends were out clubbing, I was paying the world's biggest mortgage. Determined never to have to beg for somewhere to live again. Between my neighbours' rent and my own repayments and the area booming I have more than seventy per cent equity. So maybe we'll end up closer to equal?'

'You were so scathing about my money.'

She shrugged. 'It was so fun do to. That's the real me. You may want to reconsider…'

'I wouldn't want to do this with anyone else.'

That raised the tiny ghost of the past. 'You did want to do this with someone else, once.'

He considered her seriously. 'It took me a really long time to get to the place where I could be objective about Lara. About the whole sorry mess. But our relationship was always about me making allowances for her, and she loved *that*, she didn't love me. She did me the biggest favour in getting out before it was too late.'

Just as Dan had. 'I understand.'

'Yes. I think you do.'

They kissed again, stepping back out of the view of the viewing window between studios.

'You were so right about how I treat people at work. To keep them at a distance. And my running. All designed to stop me from having to interact with anyone emotionally. And then you came along.'

'And bullied my way in?'

'And looked deep inside me and accepted who I was.'

She beamed up at him. 'Well, aren't we a pair of lucky-to-have-found-each-others?'

He smiled. 'Yeah. We really are.'

'Mr Rush?' The producer's voice boomed out over the studio PA system. Georgia could hear music in the background and knew the segment was over.

She was free.

Free to love the best man in the world.

Zander crossed to the panel and pressed a blue button. 'Yes?'

Just as fearsome as ever, despite the monumental scene he'd just made in front of his whole staff. His tone must have worked because she spoke to him with more courtesy than Georgia had heard from her all afternoon.

'*Nigel Westerly* is on line two, Mr Rush.'

She said it with the same awe she would have used if the Queen of England had picked up the phone.

Zander glanced down at the flashing light on the console, then back at Georgia. He pressed the blue button.

'Tell Westerly I'm busy.'

And then he stepped away from the panel, towards her. The last thing she saw as his head swooped back down for another kiss was the gaping dread on the face of the producer at having to tell the head of the entire network he wasn't going to get his way. And the secret smile on the face of the work-experience kid.

'That was terrible,' she whispered up at him between kisses.

'God, it felt good, though. Never did like her.'

'They aren't all bad.'

'No, they're not. I'm thinking of taking Casey with me, in fact. I'll need a bomb-proof business partner.'

'You think she'll come?'

'I have a way with women.'

'Cocky.'

'I got you, didn't I?'

'Yeah,' she breathed against his lips. 'You absolutely did.'

\* \* \* \* \*

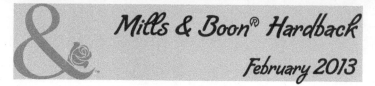

*Mills & Boon® Hardback*

*February 2013*

# ROMANCE

| | |
|---|---|
| **Sold to the Enemy** | Sarah Morgan |
| **Uncovering the Silveri Secret** | Melanie Milburne |
| **Bartering Her Innocence** | Trish Morey |
| **Dealing Her Final Card** | Jennie Lucas |
| **In the Heat of the Spotlight** | Kate Hewitt |
| **No More Sweet Surrender** | Caitlin Crews |
| **Pride After Her Fall** | Lucy Ellis |
| **Living the Charade** | Michelle Conder |
| **The Downfall of a Good Girl** | Kimberly Lang |
| **The One That Got Away** | Kelly Hunter |
| **Her Rocky Mountain Protector** | Patricia Thayer |
| **The Billionaire's Baby SOS** | Susan Meier |
| **Baby out of the Blue** | Rebecca Winters |
| **Ballroom to Bride and Groom** | Kate Hardy |
| **How To Get Over Your Ex** | Nikki Logan |
| **Must Like Kids** | Jackie Braun |
| **The Brooding Doc's Redemption** | Kate Hardy |
| **The Son that Changed his Life** | Jennifer Taylor |

# MEDICAL

| | |
|---|---|
| **An Inescapable Temptation** | Scarlet Wilson |
| **Revealing The Real Dr Robinson** | Dianne Drake |
| **The Rebel and Miss Jones** | Annie Claydon |
| **Swallowbrook's Wedding of the Year** | Abigail Gordon |

*Mills & Boon® Large Print*
*February 2013*

# ROMANCE

| | |
|---|---|
| Banished to the Harem | Carol Marinelli |
| Not Just the Greek's Wife | Lucy Monroe |
| A Delicious Deception | Elizabeth Power |
| Painted the Other Woman | Julia James |
| Taming the Brooding Cattleman | Marion Lennox |
| The Rancher's Unexpected Family | Myrna Mackenzie |
| Nanny for the Millionaire's Twins | Susan Meier |
| Truth-Or-Date.com | Nina Harrington |
| A Game of Vows | Maisey Yates |
| A Devil in Disguise | Caitlin Crews |
| Revelations of the Night Before | Lynn Raye Harris |

# HISTORICAL

| | |
|---|---|
| Two Wrongs Make a Marriage | Christine Merrill |
| How to Ruin a Reputation | Bronwyn Scott |
| When Marrying a Duke... | Helen Dickson |
| No Occupation for a Lady | Gail Whitiker |
| Tarnished Rose of the Court | Amanda McCabe |

# MEDICAL

| | |
|---|---|
| Sydney Harbour Hospital: Ava's Re-Awakening | Carol Marinelli |
| How To Mend A Broken Heart | Amy Andrews |
| Falling for Dr Fearless | Lucy Clark |
| The Nurse He Shouldn't Notice | Susan Carlisle |
| Every Boy's Dream Dad | Sue MacKay |
| Return of the Rebel Surgeon | Connie Cox |

0113 GEN STD LP

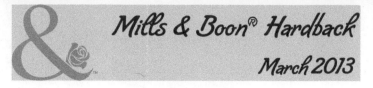
# ROMANCE

| | |
|---|---|
| **Playing the Dutiful Wife** | Carol Marinelli |
| **The Fallen Greek Bride** | Jane Porter |
| **A Scandal, a Secret, a Baby** | Sharon Kendrick |
| **The Notorious Gabriel Diaz** | Cathy Williams |
| **A Reputation For Revenge** | Jennie Lucas |
| **Captive in the Spotlight** | Annie West |
| **Taming the Last Acosta** | Susan Stephens |
| **Island of Secrets** | Robyn Donald |
| **The Taming of a Wild Child** | Kimberly Lang |
| **First Time For Everything** | Aimee Carson |
| **Guardian to the Heiress** | Margaret Way |
| **Little Cowgirl on His Doorstep** | Donna Alward |
| **Mission: Soldier to Daddy** | Soraya Lane |
| **Winning Back His Wife** | Melissa McClone |
| **The Guy To Be Seen With** | Fiona Harper |
| **Why Resist a Rebel?** | Leah Ashton |
| **Sydney Harbour Hospital: Evie's Bombshell** | Amy Andrews |
| **The Prince Who Charmed Her** | Fiona McArthur |

# MEDICAL

| | |
|---|---|
| **NYC Angels: Redeeming The Playboy** | Carol Marinelli |
| **NYC Angels: Heiress's Baby Scandal** | Janice Lynn |
| **St Piran's: The Wedding!** | Alison Roberts |
| **His Hidden American Beauty** | Connie Cox |

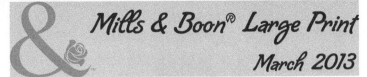

# Mills & Boon® Large Print
## March 2013

# ROMANCE

| | |
|---|---|
| A Night of No Return | Sarah Morgan |
| A Tempestuous Temptation | Cathy Williams |
| Back in the Headlines | Sharon Kendrick |
| A Taste of the Untamed | Susan Stephens |
| The Count's Christmas Baby | Rebecca Winters |
| His Larkville Cinderella | Melissa McClone |
| The Nanny Who Saved Christmas | Michelle Douglas |
| Snowed in at the Ranch | Cara Colter |
| Exquisite Revenge | Abby Green |
| Beneath the Veil of Paradise | Kate Hewitt |
| Surrendering All But Her Heart | Melanie Milburne |

# HISTORICAL

| | |
|---|---|
| How to Sin Successfully | Bronwyn Scott |
| Hattie Wilkinson Meets Her Match | Michelle Styles |
| The Captain's Kidnapped Beauty | Mary Nichols |
| The Admiral's Penniless Bride | Carla Kelly |
| Return of the Border Warrior | Blythe Gifford |

# MEDICAL

| | |
|---|---|
| Her Motherhood Wish | Anne Fraser |
| A Bond Between Strangers | Scarlet Wilson |
| Once a Playboy… | Kate Hardy |
| Challenging the Nurse's Rules | Janice Lynn |
| The Sheikh and the Surrogate Mum | Meredith Webber |
| Tamed by her Brooding Boss | Joanna Neil |